NOTHING HIDDEN

By Paulette Bullinger

Printed by United Printing
Bismarck, ND USA

Foreword

I'm a sucker for tragic death.

When I first sat down with Paulette Bullinger in 2011 and heard her plan for the book that became *Nothing Hidden*, I couldn't believe how great the story was. I mean, I could believe the premise—it was a classic cold case murder-mystery, complete with an innocent victim, romantic triangles, bootlegging, poison, and a poker hand of suspects. She had connections to historical figures that inspired her fictionalized account. She had photos. She had newspaper clippings and letters.

Nothing Hidden is fiction, but it's fiction informed by history, and the characters are inspired by an incident in a small hamlet in North Dakota involving the actual death of a young woman after a community dance in the early years of the last century. Paulette imagines what might have really happened in that small community all those years ago, and takes our hand to lead us back in time to watch. On the way, she describes a way of life that has all but vanished and exposes the dark underside of that life. Secrets upon secrets, buried for years in the unmarked grave of rural history. But by the end of our journey, nothing is left hidden at all. That it's all written down by a woman as sweet and funny as Paulette Bullinger only makes it lovelier.

Jamieson Ridenhour

Author, *Barking Mad* (Typecast, 2011)

Acknowledgements

In 2011, I attended the Red Cross Ruby Force annual fundraiser in Bismarck, North Dakota. The fundraiser included a chance to win a lifelong dream project and to work with a true professional. I won that evening, and as a result, was able to pursue an item on my "bucket list": the dream of writing a novel.

First and foremost, I want to thank my coach and mentor through the writing project, Jamieson Ridenhour, author of *Barking Mad* (Typecast, 2011). His time, patience, and guidance will forever be greatly appreciated.

I want to thank my employer, Pat Finken, for his generosity in purchasing the fundraiser tickets, and my teammates at Odney, who encouraged and supported me, from reading the manuscript to designing the cover. Among those were Meghann Theurer, Paul Kadrmas, Sherry Lillis, Donnell Dennis Roehrich, Cindy Bittner, and cover designer, Jeanne Nelson.

As the story developed, there were others who gave me invaluable feedback, including my daughter-in-law, Erica Melchior, and longtime friends, Karen Gayton Comcau and Dee Scott.

When the 2012 Red Cross Ruby Force fundraiser date drew near, I was given many public media opportunities to promote the fundraiser and to tell about my dream. Among those were KFYR-AM Radio, Prairie Public Radio, and KFYR TV. I appreciate Marnie Butcher Piehl, an organizer for the fundraiser, for her support during public appearances.

Because of a news story by reporter Michelle San Miguel on KFYR, I was put in contact with Knuckledown Press. I want to thank Ryan Christiansen for the work he put into editing and publishing the story.

Lastly, there are those closest to me, who were so important to this dream. My mother, Donna Miller, taught me the love of reading and that you are never too old to pursue your dreams. All of my children and grandchildren inspire me with their energy, especially Bailey Jo.

I want to thank my husband, Bob, who loves and supports me in all things.

All characters appearing in this work are fictitious. Any resemblance to real persons, living or dead, is purely coincidental.

For Red Cross Volunteers everywhere, who give of their time and energy for others.

NOTHING HIDDEN

Wedding Day
Spring 1912

L illian stepped out of the courthouse through heavy brass doors. She paused a moment to enjoy the warmth of the sun on her face. Today was the beginning of a whole new life.

She clung to Rueben's arm as they walked briskly toward the waiting black auto. The newlywed couple dodged rice thrown by their friends, and Lillian suspiciously believed that so many were in attendance only out of curiosity and for the celebration dinner to follow.

It was April 10, 1912, the Wednesday after Easter, and the date also marked the day when Lillian was supposed to be in another wedding as the Matron of Honor. Lillian was determined to make this the happiest day of her life.

However, the ceremony was far from what she had planned in her dreams. Non-existent was a lovely white wedding dress made of lace or her prayer book covered by a spray of flowers and carried in lace-gloved hands. She wore no gauzy white veil held in place by a hat with flower petals surrounding it. Gazing down at her simple black taffeta jacket and skirt, Lillian frowned at her choice of wedding dress. It was more suitable for a funeral. But remembering she was happy, she turned her eyes toward her new husband, Rueben, who politely nodded in the direction of their guests. His mouth showed no hint of a smile, and the plain black jacket and trousers he wore were not what she had envisioned for her groom. Lillian knew he had better options to wear than what he chose. She had arranged his closet herself!

Moreover, she knew that Rueben owned a wonderful formal suit with tails, pin-striped trousers, and a top hat. This vexed her, and she wanted to scowl, because she noticed Rueben hadn't even bothered with a vest.

Lillian would have preferred to have married in the church, but due to recent events, she couldn't chance waiting for a formal affair, and because of church doctrine, Fr. Logan would never marry her to a known Protestant. When all the recent scandal becomes past history, and after Rueben finishes formal religious training, they will hold a grand church wedding that will out do any the town of St. Giles has seen in the past. She imagines her parents and Rueben's in the first pew, and her father proudly giving her away.

Shaken back to reality, Lillian agonizes about marrying without their parents' blessings or presence. The afternoon's pitiful civil ceremony was necessary to concrete her marriage and future plans. Lillian quelled thoughts of what should have been, and focused on the future. As soon as Rueben and the new Mrs. Rueben Muester would return home, they would begin to plan their family. Lillian wanted children, lots of them, and the grand, new home they'd started to build before all the trouble began was near completion. Lillian looked forward to spending their wedding night there, and she had plans for the new home, with flowers and trees and a wonderful garden.

With these thoughts, and before she would seat herself into the auto, the new Mrs. Muester turned toward Rueben for a brief kiss. He turned his head at the moment their lips would have met, and he brushed her cheek with his, whispering in her ear. Lillian prayed the flush that his words brought to her cheeks would appear to their guests as a bride's timid reaction to her lover's amorous words, instead of seething anger, which boiled inside her.

The Envelope
1967

Catherine heard her great aunt calling her name. "I'm on my way, Auntie!" she called back, and then skipped from behind the small country store, where she lived. The long wooden structure had an apartment attached to the back, and a large cotton-wood tree provided shade for reading novels in the afternoon.

Catherine's great aunt was called Auntie (pronounced Ant-tee) by everyone who knew her, but her full name was Lillian Muester. Widowed and elderly, she lived alone and often needed assistance with some small task in her house or around her large flower garden.

"Auntie, what is it?" Catherine asked as she approached.

Auntie whispered, "I need to give you something. I have been meaning to do this for a while."

"Okay, Auntie." Catherine encouraged her great aunt and sat close to her in the garden. "What do you want to give me?" She secretly hoped it might be one of Auntie's many collectibles, and in her excitement, she interrupted, "Auntie, do you remember when you had visitors from Germany? I remember them! I have always loved the little Hummel figurines they brought for you."

"I know, Catherine," Auntie said, "but I have something much more important to give you."

Catherine was proud of the fact her Auntie was very well-known, and always having many visitors. The most interesting guests were local clergy, and on Sunday afternoons, following Mass, the priest from a neighboring town and the local priest, Fr. Williams, would come to her house late in the afternoon for a game of Canasta, a rummy-like card game that was becoming more popular than Bridge in the area.

Catherine gazed at her tiny aged great aunt, so different from all the other older "nanas" in the small town of St. Giles, south of Mandan, North Dakota, which was the county seat of Morton County. St. Giles was a sleepy little village on the west side of the Missouri River, near rolling, plateau-like hills. And while it had been a bustling little community in its heyday, the town now had only a Catholic church, a one-room school, a tavern, a grocery store, and several private homes.

Auntie's voice interrupted Catherine's thoughts. "Catherine," she said, "I have wanted to give you this for a while now, but I wanted you to grow up some, before I did."

"Auntie, I am sixteen," Catherine said, "I can take good care of anything you give me." She crossed her fingers behind her back and still hoped that Auntie was going to offer her one of the darling little Hummel figurines.

Wistful, Auntie's eyes wandered around the yard. "Catherine, just smell those lilacs. Rueben and I planted them after we built our house." Lilac bushes completely surrounded the house. "My, it's warm out here for this time of year," she said. "I can hardly catch my breath." Auntie fanned herself with a hanky, and the fragrance of lilacs hung in the air.

Catherine drew in a deep breath. Her thoughts wandered to memories of Uncle Rueben. It didn't seem so terribly long ago when he would hobble around the yard with his cane on a day like today. His death was her first experience with someone close to her passing away. Catherine tried to console Auntie whenever Auntie became sad about her past memories of him.

"Auntie, I still remember Uncle Rueben walking around this yard, trimming a branch here and there," she said. "And Daddy would try to be patient with him when he came over to the store to help out, but Uncle Rueben would always try to take over. I miss him."

Uncle Rueben was Auntie's second husband, and family gatherings were the time when Auntie's past history would be reviewed by the family, when Auntie wasn't present. Catherine had learned that Auntie had been widowed by her first husband, Josef Schmitz, when she was only eighteen. He'd been in a horrible accident with a horse and lost his leg. He never fully recovered and, eventually, he died one night in his sleep. Catherine felt as if she knew Josef through the stories that Auntie told about him, but Uncle Rueben was the only uncle that Catherine knew as Auntie's husband.

"Auntie, you really have me curious," she said, becoming impatient.

Auntie held Catherine at arm's length. She looked into her eyes as if she was looking into her soul, and her expression became serious, almost sad. "Catherine," she said, "that's the reason I'm going to give you today what I've wanted to give to you for a long time. You have a wonderful sense of curiosity, but I think you will hold this secret until the right time. When that time comes, you will find a way to reveal the truth, and the truth will set poor souls free. Anyway, that's what my old friend Anna always said: 'No rest without truth.'"

That's when Catherine noticed the small brown envelope that Auntie had tucked into her apron pocket. Catherine had never seen Auntie without her apron on, except for when she dressed for Mass.

Catherine felt a bit uncomfortable about how serious Auntie had become. She tried to lighten the conversation and to wiggle away from Auntie's grip. "Auntie," she said, "I was thinking about Uncle Rueben. Why was he always so quiet? Was he that way when you met him? I know he had a hard time talking after the stroke, but if he was such a good salesman and almost in the legislature, he must have been quite a talker before the stroke."

Auntie chuckled. "Your Uncle Rueben had what they call a 'silver tongue,'" she said. "He knew what to say, and when to say it. It still breaks my heart to think of him having nothing to live for but playing endless games of Solitaire. To watch such an active man whose only hope in life was to beat an imaginary person at cards was so hard to see over the years. Do you know that he went so far as to give the imaginary person a name? He called him Ben, for reasons of his own."

Catherine listened as Auntie went on about her favorite topic, as though mesmerized. "What a salesman your Uncle Rueben was!" she said. "He could sell leather to a cow! And how lucky I am that he chose me as his wife. He could have had any young woman he wanted and, trust me, there were some who would have done anything to win his heart. He could have been a state senator, too, if it hadn't been for his slight stroke back in 1930. After his last big stroke, the one that paralyzed his right side, your Daddy bought the store from him. My, it was so hard for your uncle to give up the business."

That is how Catherine and her family had come to live in St. Giles in the small living quarters attached to the store. Their family of six crowded into five rooms with no indoor toilet, which was another reason Catherine was a frequent visitor to Auntie's house. Auntie had a lovely modern "convenience."

Catherine followed Auntie to her favorite spot in the large yard, a small bench in her flower garden. "Auntie, what flowers will you place on the altar at church this weekend?" she asked. "Will it be the daisies?"

"No," Auntie said. "This Sunday, I want to really impress Fr. William's mother. I am inviting her down to the house after Mass for cards and for dinner. I think I will cut the tiger lilies. Would you like to come over after Mass to meet the visitors?"

Catherine nodded yes, distracted by the view. She admired the beautiful cottonwood trees that had been planted in straight rows that now arched overhead to create a natural cathedral ceiling.

Auntie went on. "Catherine," she said. "I have been thinking a lot about the past lately. Do you remember me telling you that I wanted to renew my wedding vows someday with Uncle Rueben? Our wedding was lacking something that I never could put my finger on. Maybe it happened too soon after a very bad experience for your uncle, and I always thought that renewing our wedding vows would fill something that had been missing. Sadly, that day never came."

Catherine listened respectfully as Auntie rambled on, caught up in the past. "Do you know that sometimes I dream that Rueben and I are all dressed up in our wedding clothes?" she asked. "He is in his double-breasted, pin-striped suit with tails, and in his high white collar shirt and tie. I am wearing a lovely white taffeta dress with lace at the sleeves and collar. I have a beautiful wide brimmed white hat with a veil covering my eyes, and I'm carrying my white prayer book. All the guests are friends and family from my past. The dream always starts out so lovely, and then it turns into a nightmare: After Fr. Logan pronounces us man and wife, the guests and the priest begin to laugh hysterically. Suddenly, I wake up in a cold sweat. That nightmare is the reason why every day, when I go to Mass, I take a fresh bouquet of flowers arranged from the garden. It is especially important that I put them at the Virgin's statue. Fr. Williams tells me this will protect me from demons."

"Auntie," Catherine said softly, trying to change the subject and cheer her up. "You grow the most beautiful flowers. You have them planted so they bloom at all different times of the year. Early in the spring, there are tulips and irises. Late in the fall, there are sunflowers and goldenrods."

"Yes," Auntie replied, her eyes following the sweeping movement of Catherine's hand. "I love all kinds of flowers, except for those horrible roses. What kind of flowers would want to cause you pain when you picked them? That is why I never planted roses near to my other flowers, but Rueben insisted on planting them anyway, and so he planted them next to the shed at the back of the store. Look, see how they have spread and grow wild over there?" Auntie grumbled, pointing at a lovely spread of red and yellow blossoms.

"Do you know why I say small prayers when I pick flowers?" Auntie asked. "These little prayers are indulgences for some poor soul to be released more quickly from suffering in Purgatory, as encouraged by the church. I have so many people to pray for." She sighed. "Some prayers are good for 500 days less suffering," she said. "Catherine, please pray for me every day when I am gone. Will you promise?" Her shaking, withered hand, mottled with age spots and dried with time, handed Catherine the envelope, her simple golden wedding band glinting in the warm afternoon sun. The envelope was small and yellowed with age and with Do Not Destroy written in small cursive letters on the front.

Tucked inside the envelope was a newspaper clipping, crumbling, and equally yellowed with age.

Finally getting to the point, Auntie began to explain the contents of the envelope to Catherine. Her story sounded like a tale right out of Catherine's favorite kind of book, a mystery novel, and Catherine imagined herself a kind of sleuth out to solve some big mystery, a real Nancy Drew.

After she finished her story, Auntie cautioned, "Catherine, this tragedy was something that happened when I was a young woman and not much older than you. I don't want the contents of this envelope ever to be forgotten. Will you promise to never forget what I'm telling you? Promise me that you'll never tell anyone else about this until I'm long gone. This will be a secret between you and me until the right time." Auntie whispered as though someone else was within earshot, and added, "Catherine, there will be a key to unlock the real truth. No one else must know this but you. When the time comes, use the key to reveal all of the truth."

"Auntie, I promise," Catherine whispered, although there was no one who could have possibly overheard their conversation. "I will take good care of your secret."

Catherine held her Auntie's hand for a moment and watched as a tear slipped from Auntie's eye. It landed on Catherine's hand as though sealing an oath.

Farewell Auntie
1967

Carrying Auntie's secret was difficult for Catherine. Nothing much mysterious ever happened in that little prairie town of less than sixty people on a given day. Catherine had lived next door to Auntie all her young life, and Auntie had never revealed a secret like this before, even though she'd shared plenty of secrets with the young girl.

A few weeks after receiving the envelope, Catherine noticed that Daddy was at Auntie's house most of an afternoon. "Auntie is not feeling well," Momma explained. "Her heart has been racing again." Catherine and Momma waited and watched out the kitchen window, which faced Auntie's large, beautiful garden.

When Daddy emerged from the house, his elderly aunt clutched his arm. Momma and Catherine moved to cross over to Auntie's yard to see if they could help in any way, and Catherine heard Auntie whisper to Daddy, "Martin, take me around the yard. I want to see the flowers and the trees one more time." As Catherine watched, Daddy tenderly took Auntie around the yard, stopping briefly here and there so that she could touch a delphinium, or smell a hollyhock.

Daddy said to Auntie, "Come now, we must get you to the hospital." Slowly, they walked through the flowers and around the white frame house with red trim and the screened-in front porch. The church and the parsonage were just up the hill from Auntie's house, and after a few moments, Fr. Williams came walking briskly into the yard. He was a frequent visitor, and so his visits were not unusual, but today he had a concerned look on his face and he appeared to be hurried. When he reached Daddy and Auntie, he took Auntie by the hands.

Catherine watched Daddy as he walked toward the garage. She heard the gears grind on the old Chevy as he backed out, and Fr. Williams and Auntie sat on her garden bench and waited for him to pull the car in front of the ornate, iron scroll gate that led into her large yard. Fr. Williams tenderly brushed back the hair on Auntie's forehead and tucked it into the hairnet she always wore. Daddy helped Auntie into the back seat.

Catherine thought it strange that Fr. Williams moved into the back seat next to Auntie. He carried a small prayer book and a little black pouch. Momma and Catherine heard Auntie tease Fr. Williams. "What's in the little pouch, Father?" she asked. "I'm sure it's not your set of Canasta cards!" With a quick move, Fr. Williams pulled the bottom part of his cassock into the car and pulled the door shut.

Auntie motioned Catherine over to the car and to open the rear door on Auntie's side. She whispered, taking time to catch her breath between words. "Catherine, remember your promise. No secret-telling for a very long time."

"Yes, Auntie," Catherine said. "My lips are sealed. I will see you tomorrow."

Fr. Williams gave Catherine a questioning glance.

After the car disappeared down the road, Catherine had an inexplicable feeling of sadness. She went to her room and looked at the little envelope tucked safely in her diary, and sprawled across her bed, feeling the softness of the chenille coverlet. She smiled to think of the past Sunday afternoon, when Fr. Williams and the priest from across the hills visited Auntie for a game of Canasta and a shot of whiskey and plenty of cigar smoking. She'd been invited to visit, because Fr. William's mother was going to be one of the guests, and Auntie thought Catherine could keep her entertained and keep the nut and candy dishes filled. Mostly, Catherine joined them because she liked the smell of the spicy cigars. She could barely see across the room because of the heavy blue haze caused by all the smoke.

Catherine had begun to worry about Auntie that afternoon. She had coughed and pounded her chest through the whole game. Meanwhile, Catherine found the small-town gossip during the card game to be especially juicy. She heard about an exorcism performed down the road at the old Anna Crow Wing house, and it gave her a kind of fun creepy feeling. It seems there was some pesky poltergeist bothering the renters living there.

Before the priests had left that Sunday evening, Auntie requested, "Fr. Williams, can you give me a special blessing? Pray something that will pack some punch in Purgatory!"

Fr. Williams smiled and agreed. He placed both hands on Auntie's head and prayed as she bowed. Her cough interrupted the prayer before it was finished, and Fr. Williams said she received a partial indulgence from that prayer, which meant that just a small portion of any temporary punishment in Purgatory due to her sins would be removed.

Auntie looked pale. Catherine understood why. She knew her Catechism well enough to know that if you received a plenary indulgence and died at that instant, you would fly right into Heaven, but with a partial indulgence, you weren't going to Heaven anytime soon.

Late that night, Catherine heard Daddy come into the house and go into his bedroom, shutting the door behind him. She heard him speak in a low voice to Momma. He said, "Elaine, Auntie didn't even make the trip into town. She grabbed her chest about halfway into Mandan and said she couldn't breathe. Fr. Williams pulled out his Extreme Unction oils and was able to give the last rites just in time."

Momma cried softly, and then came into Catherine's bedroom. "Catherine," Momma whispered, "Auntie has been called to Heaven by Jesus."

Catherine wasn't so sure, and cried herself to sleep.

The next evening, when Daddy and Momma returned home after making funeral arrangements, Daddy called the family into the living room for rosary. He began by asking for the saints to "lead all souls to Heaven, especially the soul of Auntie."

Catherine turned to Momma, questioning. "I thought you said Auntie went home to be with Jesus?"

Daddy consoled her. "This was just in case."

Just in case what, Catherine wondered, but she knew it best not to question Daddy anymore.

The day of the funeral was preceded by two days of lengthy wake services, with seemingly endless rosaries from all the different Roman Catholic groups to which Auntie belonged. After a Requiem Mass, Fr. Williams led the somber procession up the dirt road from the church to the cemetery.

As the funeral line moved down the dusty path toward the cemetery, Catherine remembered things she and Auntie had done together. Catherine was the eldest in her family, and with Auntie being childless, she'd become like a second mother to Catherine. She remembered how adventurous Auntie had always been: She rode a horse until her hips started giving her trouble, and Daddy said she was the only woman who played tennis and who drove her own car before it became popular with women. Auntie had spent hours hiking and looking for herbs and natural medicines in the hills and along the river, and she told stories of how much she had learned about Lakota medicine from her friend, Anna. Auntie had begun to teach Catherine some of the homemade medicines before she became ill.

One particular memory came to mind as Catherine looked down the hill from the church. She recalled how Auntie loved to turn the engine off in her old blue car when they came home from daily Mass early in the morning. She would allow the car to roll down the hill from the church to "save gas," she said, but Catherine believed she performed the odd action because it was fun.

As these thoughts came back to her, and with so many of them funny, Catherine couldn't help but giggle as she walked to the cemetery, which caused Daddy to give her a very stern look.

The procession gathered around Auntie's coffin for the final prayers.

Deus, cujus miseratióne ánimæ fidélium requiéscunt, hunc túmulum benedícere dignáre, eíque Angelum tuum sanctum députa custódem... Per Christum Dóminum nostrum. Amen.

Fr. Williams prayed loudly as he circled the grave, and the chain rattled against the brass censor as he waved it over and over above the coffin. A sweet, musky-smelling smoke floated above the open grave. Next, he circled the coffin with a holy water sprinkler, and this time he spoke in English as he sprinkled, so that the mourners could answer. "Eternal rest, grant unto her, O Lord!" he pronounced loudly, and the people responded, "And let perpetual light shine upon her!"

Fr. Williams continued, "May her soul, and the souls of all the faithful departed, through the mercy of God, rest in peace! Amen."

During prayers, Catherine felt confused. Where in the world, Heaven, or Purgatory, was Auntie? Was she suffering? Was she resting somewhere?

Some things are so mystifying. Catherine's tears rolled down her cheeks as the pallbearers lowered Auntie's coffin into the ground between the graves of her first and second husbands. Auntie's baby boy had been buried just outside the cemetery fence, because he hadn't been baptized, stillborn at birth. Auntie had tried to explain this to Catherine, but it made Auntie sad, and so Catherine stopped asking why. The little baby couldn't possibly have sinned, born dead. Looking toward that little white marker with just a name and a date, Catherine felt sad that the only flowers on the grave were the dead ones that someone had carelessly thrown over the barbed wire fence from a previous funeral. Catherine resolved in her mind that after everyone had left the cemetery, she would give Baby Adam (named after Adam in the Bible) the fresh bouquet of flowers that she'd placed on his mother's grave, some late summer yellow lilies from Auntie's garden. Catherine had said the little prayers that she'd promised Auntie she would repeat while gathering flowers, and after everyone had left the cemetery, she strolled around the graves before running down the hill to Auntie's house.

The family was going to eat a meal, read Auntie's will, and divide up her personal belongings, but Catherine had no desire to see Auntie's things sifted through as though there was some type of flea market going on at her house. Instead, Catherine felt it was necessary to visit the graves of those whose secret she would one day share, and it took some searching outside the cemetery to find the rounded Indian burial mound with just a small field rock on top and with the name Anna scratched into it. Catherine placed wildflowers from the surrounding prairie onto Anna's grave, because wildflowers seemed more appropriate from what she knew about her.

When Catherine returned to Auntie's house, someone placed a

Hummel in her hands, a little figurine of a girl baking, the prized porcelain piece she had always dreamt of owning, and told her that Auntie had painted Catherine's name and a note onto it, a Bible verse, Luke 12:2.

The years went by, and Catherine saved the yellowed envelope. She waited for the right time to keep the promise that she'd made to Auntie that day in the garden. As she moved from city to city, and house to house, she always kept that little envelope somewhere safe. She kept it in a small box with the fragile little Hummel, because she feared that leaving the figurine outside the box might cause the already pastel colors to fade, or some mishap might cause it to break. Every now and then, she would read the story on the newspaper clipping, and she would look at the Hummel to remind her of Auntie, and chuckle to remember how she was always so concerned about her reputation while she walked this earth. Before she died, Auntie had seemed so adamant about the concept of Truth, and how it might free her soul, alongside all the intercessory prayers.

As the problems and cares of her own life took priority, the adult Catherine began to think less and less of her childhood promise to Auntie. Only on the yearly anniversary of Auntie's death did she remember how, sometime in the future, she was to tell the truth about that most wicked of mortal sins—that she was to tell the truth about the murder.

The Scandalous News
1910

R ose Welsley struggled to keep her dress from crumpling as she rode along in the rear seat of the Model T. As they drew closer to Bismarck, she grew more impatient to see Lillian.

Lillian Kruenfel and her family lived on the west side of the Missouri River, just outside of St. Giles. The Welsley family lived on the east side of the river and farmed near Rivers Edge. The families lived nearly across the river from each other, and they would visit when the river was frozen and they could easily walk or drive sleighs, buggies, or autos across on the ice. In summer, a local fisherman, Old Joe, would ferry people from one side to the other for socializing, shopping or church activities, and the Welsleys and Kruenfels had arranged to meet as often as they could, either in St. Giles or in Rivers Edge, but meeting in Bismarck was the highlight of their summer.

Early in the spring, Rose and Lillian began making plans for their summer meeting in Bismarck by staying in contact through letters. On occasion, the young ladies could see each other from opposite sides of the river while picking chokecherries or while checking fishing set-lines along the riverbank. They would wave and call to each other across the water, and laugh at the echoes that their voices made.

Now on her way to Bismarck, Rose occupied the time by recalling the unbelievable letter she had received from Lillian earlier in the spring. This would be her first opportunity to see Lillian since she'd received the letter.

My dearest friend Rose,

Oh how I wish I could tell you this news face to face. I pray you will still consider me to be your best friend once you read my news.

Do you remember my beau, Josef Schmitz? I am now his wife. I was not planning to be married this soon, but, oh, saints in Heaven, how do I tell you this? Josef and I are going to have a baby!

I had to tell my Ma and Pa. Oh dear, I never heard such screaming as from my Ma. She nearly fainted. My Pa became so angry, I ran out of the house. Josef was waiting outside. Pa took us by the arms, from which I still have a bruise, and pulled us up to the church. There, we were each made to go into the confessional, and Fr. Logan asked for our confessions. They lasted longer than I remember anyone I have seen go to confession. Fr. Logan wanted every secret detail confessed so that we would not commit the sin of sacrilege. I was so ashamed to say everything, and then he gave us so many prayers in penance. After that, he asked for our wedding vows, but because the Holy Eucharist was in the church, he would not marry us there. We had to go next door to the parsonage and get married in the parlor.

Oh, dear friend, I am so sorry. I know we had dreamed of someday being each other's Matron of Honor. Will you ever forgive me? Will you be my child's Godmother when he or she is born? Will that make up for my failure to live up to our girlhood promises?

My parents have not spoken to me since that day. I am heartbroken, but very much in love with Josef and looking forward to my new family.

Friends for Eternity,
Lillian ~~Kruenfel~~ Schmitz

After Rose had allowed her parents to read the letter, Welsley family visits to the Kruenfels in St. Giles suddenly ceased.

Rose sobbed all night after reading the letter. She had a difficult time believing that Lillian was being treated so harshly by her family, and she decided what was done, was done. She would always be Lillian's friend, and although they were the best of friends, Rose secretly envied Lillian, because Lillian was extremely daring and had big dreams about the future. She wanted to vote, she created a tennis court in her back yard, she loved to ride the wildest horses, and she could drive an auto. She also enjoyed smoking tobacco and wearing men's pants. All this independence and Lillian was only seventeen years old.

Rose never thought of Lillian as a beauty, but she always had a wonderful look of mischief about her. The only photograph Rose had of Lillian was taken when they were in Bismarck in the fall of 1909. The families had met in the city for the St. Mary's Fall Festival, and a traveling photographer passing through Bismarck set up a makeshift studio in a tent to capitalize on the farmers' harvest income.

The whole idea for the photograph had been Papa's. He wanted a family photograph, and so Mama, Papa, Anton, and herself, were required to sit very still until the image developed on the camera's plate. In the back of the tent, Lillian and her family waited for a photo session that day, as well, and it had been difficult for Rose to remain sober-faced because Lillian made faces at Rose to get her to smile, and all the while Lillian stood next to the young photographer and fluttered her eyelashes at him.

The family photograph had taken several weeks to reach the Welsley family by mail. Rose remembered Papa's reaction when he opened the package and grimaced at the photograph. He scoffed, "It is what it is, but look at my most beautiful Rose!" And Mama's face looked like she was in pain, her hand clutching a handkerchief, because prior to the photo session, she'd had one of her crying spells. Papa looked stoic and uncomfortable, and Anton had moved and his face looked blurred.

Looking at the photograph, Rose had to admit she really didn't recognize herself, but secretly, she enjoyed a moment of sinful pride.

If I had to describe the woman who is staring back at me, I would have to say she is quite beautiful, she thought.

Papa had allowed Rose to have a picture taken of her alone, too, and Lillian's parents allowed the same, so that the girls could exchange photographs. During the session, Rose believed the handsome young man had been trying to seek her attention, regardless of Lillian's attempts to distract him. She remembered him saying, "Rose, what a lovely name," and then he produced a rose from somewhere and handed it to her to hold in the photograph. He bent down close and whispered near her ear, and pretended to control a stray strand of her hair. "A rose by any other name would smell as sweet," he'd said, and Rose knew from her schooling that the line was from Shakespeare's *Romeo and Juliet*. She felt a momentary feeling of warmth, but Lillian's laughter quickly brought her back to reality. Lillian laughed and said, "Sir, that Prairie Rose does not want suitors at this time. She is planning to be a schoolteacher. As you know, schoolteachers cannot be seen in the company of young men, nor can they wed."

It was true. At sixteen years old, Rose was tall, slim, and had what some called an angelic face, and she was quiet, and painfully shy. She'd already had suitors asking Papa if they could call on her to court for the purpose of marriage, but she'd asked Papa to turn them all away. She wanted to go to school and to become a teacher. Papa had granted nearly all her requests, except for this one.

"I, on the other hand, plan to operate a business," Lillian said, "and I would like to find a handsome man to be my partner! Sir, I believe it is time for *my* photograph, but I want a more contemporary portrait. I do not want to sit in a chair as if some statue. Instead, I will place one knee on the seat and with my side to you, facing the back of the chair, with one arm across the chair back, and the other against my temple."

And so much to Rose's shock, Lillian had posed herself in this way. Rose shook off the thought that Lillian had been flamboyant. She probably didn't know the effect her actions had carried. She'd emphasized her ample bosom by raising her arms, and by leaning into the chair, her curvaceous bottom was more than noticeable. Rose had thought, There she goes again, being bold and forward. The others in the room were stunned, except for Anton, and Rose remembered how he reacted, as though he were about to pounce on her friend. What a repulsive thought, her brother wrapped in the arms of her best friend. Meanwhile the photographer, who seemed excited about being given some creative allowance beyond the traditional pose, began the session as quickly as possible, and before someone responsible might stop the action.

The most striking facet of Lillian's photograph had been the look on Lillian's face. Rose couldn't put her finger on it, but it almost looked as if she'd held a secret, much like the portrait of the Mona Lisa.

Unknown to Rose, her Papa had plans for her, but they were not what she had planned for her own life.

Bismarck was on the rebound following the fire that nearly destroyed the town in 1898. It was becoming a modern city, with merchants replacing wood buildings with brick-and-concrete structures. Shops and restaurants were opening rapidly, as were schools and government offices. A hospital had recently been built by Catholic nuns, and people were moving through the city on the railroad, mostly to South Dakota to seek their fortunes in the gold mines.

Chris Welsley expertly steered his dusty black Model T as it bumped and twisted along the dirt road leading to Bismarck. He and Mary had found a need to drive to Bismarck from their farmstead near Rivers Edge. Mary had a doctor's appointment, and they needed supplies. Today was also the one chance during the summer that their daughter, Rose, and her friend Lillian could meet for some girl chitchat.

"Rose, what time were you going to meet Lillian?" Chris asked again. "I need to get Mama to the doctor by eleven." He turned back to look at her jostling about in the rear seat. Before Rose could answer, he added, "I hope you have a good visit with Lillian, but keep it short. I have lots of supplies to check on and your Mama wants to stop at the dressmakers." Chris winked at Rose. "I am sure there will be a new dress style that you won't be able to live without."

"Oh, Papa, you dote on me too much," Rose said. "But what about Anton? Will you be bringing him a surprise home from Bismarck? After all, he did have to stay home this trip to make sure the chores get done."

"Hmph, we'll see," he replied. "Where are you meeting Lillian?"

"Right in front of the railroad station," she said.

"Rose, you know I don't really care for you standing there by yourself. Will she be waiting there for you? And I don't want you standing around there with Lillian because she is a little too friendly with the young fellas, and all those railroad men are lonely."

"Papa!" Rose said. "Lillian is married. I doubt she is being flirtatious! You know about Josef's accident. I need to cheer her up. Besides, you know that she must be starting to look… well, you know."

"What I know is that sometimes God punishes us for our sins here on earth, and I think that Josef's accident was God telling them that they had sinned."

Just then, Mary moaned. She clutched her abdomen as they hit a rough bump on the road.

After that, the family rode in silence. When Mary had one of her pain spells, she just couldn't tolerate noise, including conversations.

Chris had grown tired of all this change-of-life business, but he took his marriage vow of "in sickness and in health" seriously. After all, marriage was a sacrament of the church.

He reflected on the friendship with the Kruenfel family. They had been friends for more than five years, and met often at each other's homes for card-playing and for an occasional Sunday picnic. They'd become acquainted when both families began to attend St. Mary's Catholic Church in Bismarck before the small wooden church was built in St. Giles. Chris had spent as much free time as he could in St. Giles to help John Kruenfel build the church, and their strong Catholic faith bonded them. Coincidentally, the families had daughters the same age who became best friends, which seemed to solidify the alliance.

The twenty mile road trip gave Chris ample time to think. He'd made the decision to move to Bismarck after leaving a mining job out east. It had become terribly dangerous work, and so many miners had been killed. He thanked the good Lord he'd decided to leave and make the move to North Dakota to try his hand at farming, which is what he really wanted to do. Many of the earliest homesteaders were abandoning the hard life and moving to the city, and he thought about how fortunate he was to be able to buy up a large section of land south of Bismarck on the east side of the Missouri River. With his mechanical knowledge and a willingness to work long, hard hours, Chris had built up a beautiful farmstead. He ran a strict household, too, and had high expectations for everyone to work equally strenuous hours.

One of his stops today would be at the lumber yard. The home he'd built for his family was three stories tall. The main floor was a large kitchen with a canning room, a parlor, and a dining room. The second floor contained the family's bedrooms, and upstairs was a large attic. Today he would purchase additional decorative corner brackets for the front porch. The main construction was finished, and so it was time to add the finishing touches. He'd built a large barn for the animals and a bunkhouse for the hired hands, some of whom were Indians from the Standing Rock Indian Reservation.

They worked long hours for a decent meal and minimal pay.

As Chris pondered his accomplishments, he began to wonder how he'd handle the estate. He knew he wouldn't be able to continue working long days, and even with seasonal help his son, Anton, wouldn't be able to farm alone should something happen. There seemed to be only one possible solution: A husband for Rose.

As they pulled into town, Chris looked forward to meeting up with some of his male friends in Bismarck while the women attended to their own business. A shave and a haircut at the barbershop and a cup of coffee would be time enough to catch up with all of the latest in politics and local hearsay.

They reached the railway station and marveled at the new construction underway for the Hotel McKenzie. It was going to be a building that would change Bismarck into a modern-looking city.

Chris felt Rose tap his shoulder. "There she is!" she said.

"Rose, here I am, over here!" Lillian called from an archway in front of the Northern Pacific Railway Station.

Chris pulled the Model T as close to the depot as he could get. He gave Rose a look that she understood to mean, "Be careful, and be on your best behavior." Chris felt dismayed about Lillian and her bulging belly. He'd begun to lose respect for her the day that Rose received that letter in the mail. He turned the Model T into the dirt-packed Main Street and drove in the direction of the doctor's office.

Despite the changes to Lillian's body, Rose recognized her wild hand-wave instantly. She noticed Lillian was very obviously pregnant and she looked tired. Her face looked red and puffy, possibly from the heat.

"It is so good to see you," Rose said. "How is Josef?" She hurried to Lillian's side and embraced her carefully.

"Oh, Rose, he is not doing well," Lillian said. "The doctor said the surgeon may have to amputate his leg. Some kind of infection has set in, and his foot has begun to turn black. The doctor said if they don't remove his leg, the infection could spread and kill him. Oh, Rose, what do I do?" Lillian lowered her voice. "I have no money," she said, "and Ma and Pa won't let me move back home. They're ashamed of me. You're my only friend."

Lillian bit her lip. "I never should have allowed Josef to ride my horse," she said. "I thought the horse needed exercise, and with the baby growing inside me, I didn't want to ride. Josef was thrown from the horse almost as soon as he got on. I couldn't bear hearing his screams. I nearly fainted when I saw his mangled leg beneath him. It was a miracle there was a railroad man passing by in his auto, and he took him to the hospital. Oh, Rose, what will I do?"

Lillian broke down in sobs. Rose put her arm around her friend, and said, "I will ask my father to help, and I will pray for you. Let's have something to eat. You must keep up your strength."

Desperate Times
1910

O utside the hospital room, Lillian cried softly as she listened to Josef moan as he recovered from the effects of the chloroform. She was not allowed inside because of the danger of infection.

Just before the amputation, Josef had begged her to let him die. After his broken leg had failed to heal, gangrene had set in.

The Benedictine sisters at the hospital allowed her to work in the kitchen to pay for some of the hospital bills, and they allowed her to stay in the monastery there. Fr. Logan had heard the news of the amputation, and while he was making his rounds visiting the sick in the hospital, he met with Lillian to explain the proper burial of the amputated leg.

"Lillian, it is necessary that amputated limbs be buried in a blessed place, either in individual graves, or in a common burial area," he said. "It would be prudent for you to choose a burial plot now for you and Josef in the St. Giles cemetery. That will allow the leg to be buried properly."

"Fr. Logan," Lillian sobbed. "Why? Why such a fuss over this now?"

"Lillian, the body must be buried whole so that on Resurrection Day, the soul can be joined to the body."

Lillian had then accompanied Fr. Logan to St. Giles with the amputated leg. There he helped Lillian choose a burial plot, and he arranged for neighbors to dig a grave for the leg and to bury it. Lillian stood alongside Fr. Logan in the cemetery for graveside prayers.

After Josef was fitted for his prosthetic leg, a poorly designed, wooden one with a slipper-type shoe, the couple returned to St. Giles. To Lillian's dismay, Fr. Logan insisted that Josef should visit his leg's gravesite, and there he recited more graveside prayers.

"Fr. Logan, I have a question," Lillian asked out of earshot of Josef. "I've been thinking about all this being buried-whole-for-Resurrection-Day teaching. As I was kneeling in church one morning, saying my rosary, I remembered that the Catechism teaches that there must be bones or relics of saints in every Catholic altar. I questioned God about that. How can the saints become whole on Resurrection Day if bits and pieces of them are scattered throughout the world in various altars?"

Fr. Logan cleared his throat and fumbled for an answer, "Well, some of these things should be left up to the church to consider. You have too many other things to worry about than deep church mystery. Take Josef home and pray for his recovery. Pray for your unborn baby, as well."

Life was hard, but Lillian was able to take care of her husband by working small jobs around St. Giles. Her energy turned to the unborn infant she carried, and she took to creating a layette. Lillian found part-time employment a couple hours per day at the local mercantile as a clerk, and she also rented out their small house in St. Giles as the funeral parlor for holding pre-funeral vigils. Having a gift for growing things—a talent she learned from a local Lakota woman named Anna—she was able to grow and can food. She was also employed as a cook at a small boarding house on Saturdays. She did whatever was necessary to care for her struggling family.

Every day became more and more exhausting as she grew larger with the pregnancy. Lillian's day did not end after her jobs were finished; the chores at home needed doing, as well. Her horse, her garden, and housekeeping always waited for her because Josef was now mostly disabled.

Lillian jumped at the sound of the bell ringing from the bedroom. Why had she borrowed the school bell for Josef to summon her when he needed something?

"Josef, put the bell down, please!"

"Lillian, I need you! Come in here now!" Josef shrieked.

"What is it now, Josef?" Lillian snapped back. "I was in here a few minutes ago!"

"When I need you, I need you now!" Josef bellowed. "Get me something to drink. I'm thirsty."

"Josef, the doctor said you should be getting up to do these little things for yourself. If you don't keep moving, you'll become more disabled."

"Then the hell with it," Josef growled. "I can't live like this. How many weeks has it been, hobbling around here, having to strap my leg on? No money. No work. I'm not even able to be a husband to my wife. Nothing but pain, day after day. If the Lord is good, then He should have just let me die."

"Josef, please don't say that. I can't bear to hear it. You just have to give yourself time. When the baby comes, you'll be able to be a husband to me again, and you'll be able to work again, but you cannot lie around here and feel sorry for yourself day after day. I cannot bear to hear your mumblings anymore. Please, cheer up for my sake. I will check with Anna for something for your pain."

Anna lived just down the rutted dirt road, approximately a mile. The morning after her quarrel with Josef, Lillian walked down the road to spend time with Anna and to get some of her native healing herbs for Josef's pain. Lillian kept strong medicine from the doctor high up in her cupboard for screaming pain, but she chose to use it only when necessary, because it was very expensive.

Anna showed Lillian how to mix up a combination of wormwood sprouts, marigold flowers, sage, rosemary, and other ingredients for his pain. Lillian recalled Anna's additional words of advice: "Lillian, you, too, are going to get sick," she said. "I will mix up a medicine for your nerves. It will be safe for your baby. I can see sickness in your face. Remember, no medicine works without prayer to the Wakan Tanka."

Secretly, Lillian sat in reverence as Anna prayed to her Great Spirit. She was warned by Fr. Logan against doing so, because it was as evil as going to a Protestant church service, but Lillian was desperate, and Anna seemed the only person willing to help.

Time went by and no remedies seemed to help Josef. He became more demanding and more difficult to live with. The bell rang incessantly.

One morning, Lillian woke up to something unusual. Silence. There were no shouts to bring the bedpan. There were no demands for an extra blanket. There was no bell-ringing.

Lillian had begun sleeping on the floor next to the bed shortly after Josef had come home from the hospital so that she would be close by to answer his calls. She'd begun sleeping outside the bed because she'd accidentally kicked Josef's inflamed leg stump a couple of times, and each time Josef answered her back with a hard swat against her face. The last time he'd struck her, he'd given her a black eye. When asked about it by Anna, Lillian lied, and said she'd accidentally bumped a cupboard door at the restaurant. Anna had shaken her head in response, as if she knew full well that Lillian was lying.

"Josef! Josef!" Lillian called up from the floor. Nothing.

Lillian stood up and walked around to her own side of the bed, and knowing something was wrong, she crawled under the covers next to Josef. He was cold. Dead.

She felt her baby move. "Dear God," she said. "I am ashamed. I must be wicked. I am happy. I am happy this hell is over. Please forgive me. I will do a proper penance."

In a daze, Lillian rose out of bed and then walked down the dirt road in her nightclothes. In the early morning light, she saw Anna walk down the road toward her. Anna carried a basket.

"Anna," Lillian sobbed. "Josef will not need his medicine today."

Anna looked at Lillian sympathetically, and said, "I know. I had a vision. I'm bringing you a basket of food. You will need to keep your strength. I will get your priest for your white man's ways."

Anna went to Fr. Logan, and he came rushing into the room as Lillian sat on a chair next to the bed.

"Lillian, when did you last hear Josef?" Fr. Logan demanded.

"I went to get him a drink of water early this morning," she said. "Before the sun came up."

"It may not be too late," he said. "Sometimes, the soul can still be in the body for a couple of hours. The person may not be completely dead, even though he looks like it. I will give him the Last Rites of the Church."

"Shouldn't we find the sheriff?" Lillian asked.

"No, it is obvious that he was a sick man. We would only need to find the sheriff if he was murdered. Please, we must prepare for the final sacrament. Start by sponging down Josef's hands, face, and foot," he said and began arranging the body on the bed.

Fr. Logan stopped. "Lillian, did you administer Josef's medications?" he asked.

"Yes, Fr. Logan. Why do you ask?"

"Because of this," he said, and showed Lillian the empty bottle he'd found under Josef's pillow.

"Oh, no! That is the laudanum that was to be used only when Josef was in terrible pain! I had it on a high shelf so that Josef could not find it. How did he get it?" Lillian cried.

"That makes no difference," he said. "We must bury Josef quickly, before sundown. I will get the men in town to dig a grave. We will have no service. Finding this under his pillow will be between you and me." Fr. Logan covered Josef's face with the blanket, and appeared to evaluate the situation. "It looks to me as though he died of an accident," he said. "He may have lost track of how much medication he took. That is what I will write in the church record book. Pray for his soul."

After Fr. Logan left, Anna helped Lillian prepare the body for burial. They bathed and dressed Josef's body, and Anna brought in a small bowl that drifted sweet-smelling smoke. It smelled like the incensing ritual at Benediction. Anna chanted in her Lakota language as she walked around the room, and for some reason, it gave Lillian a sense of peace.

That afternoon, several men, members of the church, arrived and took Josef's body. They laid him in a rough rectangular box that someone had hastily made from old wood. Lillian, still in shock, followed them up the hill to the cemetery. Fr. Logan stood silent as the men lowered the rough wooden coffin into the grave, and then covered it. A few curious townspeople watched from outside the cemetery gate. Lillian snatched a handful of dirt and threw it on the box, and then for a long time she stood near the fresh-smelling black soil that covered Josef's grave. She watched the autumn sun set in red, yellow, and gold, and she felt incredibly free.

Her child moved, and she placed her hand over her bulging stomach. She whispered, "It's just you and me now. Mary, Joseph and Jesus protect us."

Death and the Grave
1910

The news of Josef's death reached Rose and her family the day after he passed away. Anna instructed Old Joe to ferry across the river to the Welsley farmstead to inform them of the death. In shock, Rose wrote a letter to Lillian saying they would come for the funeral, and she sent it back with Old Joe.

The following day, Rose and her family ferried across the river to St. Giles, expecting to attend a wake and a funeral. They were surprised to find that Josef had been buried so quickly.

Lillian covered up the reason for Josef's quick burial by saying it was because of the infection in his leg. It had become re-infected, she said, and before Josef died, it was already beginning to have a stench.

As the family visited the gravesite, Rose and Lillian held hands. Moved with compassion, Chris told Lillian that he would make an iron cross for Josef's grave marker. Mary asked if she could sing a traditional graveside song in German, and then sang, "*Das Schicksal wird keinen verschonen…*" Rose wrapped her arms around Lillian as Mary sang the sad-sounding melody. She tried to console Lillian as the young widow allowed herself tears for the first time since Josef's death. Afterward, they walked arm-in-arm down the hill to Lillian's small house, where Anna had a lunch prepared for the families.

"Rose, that song that your mother sang, what did the words mean in English?" Lillian asked.

"Lillian, that song is usually sung as the coffin is being lowered into the ground, but because we missed that, Mama wanted to sing it anyway. The words mean 'the fate that will spare no one…', meaning, we all will have this same future: death and the grave."

Rose felt relieved that her father had decided to pay Lillian's family a visit before arranging for Old Joe to ferry them back across the river. She knew her father did not approve of all the so-called sins in Lillian's life, and it cheered Rose when he took pity on Lillian. Rose prayed that he could talk some sense into John Kruenfel regarding the state Lillian was in, because Lillian was going to need family. Just before Rose and her own family left Lillian's home, Lillian faced Rose as they said farewell.

"Rose," Lillian asked, "can you stay for a while? The baby is almost due, and I don't want to be alone. Please say, 'Yes.'"

Without hesitation, Rose replied, "Yes, of course I'll stay. I'll stay until fall, but then I'm going to Bismarck to attend school. I will be living at St Mary's boarding school." She looked at her parents pleadingly, and received the nod from her father.

Rose and Lillian spent most of their time preparing for Lillian's baby. The young women lovingly sewed little shirts and blankets, and they enjoyed conversations of all kinds. Rose was amazed by Lillian's quick recovery from grief.

"Rose, do you think we should have bought some of those comet pills?" Lillian asked. "Before Halley's Comet passed by this past spring, they said it could make someone sick or behave strangely."

Rose laughed. "No, Lillian," she said, "but that peddler on the street that day in Bismarck sure made it sound as though something horrible would happen if we didn't."

"Well, maybe it was an omen," Lillian mumbled. "Something horrible did happen."

The following day in the warm, early summer morning, Rose could hear Lillian screaming in pain. She raced into the kitchen and found Lillian on the floor, a pool of blood beginning to stain her skirt.

"Rose!" Lillian screamed. "Run, get Anna!"

Rose dashed out the door and ran the mile to Anna's home. Anna was working in her garden when she heard Rose scream her name. Anna had delivered many babies, Lillian had told Rose, and Anna would be the midwife for the birth of hers. The women ran back as fast as they could and opened the door to a shocking, pathetic scene. Rose fell sick when she saw Lillian tenderly holding a small little bundle. The baby was wrapped in a white, flour sack dishtowel.

"It's a baby boy, Rose," Lillian sobbed. Rose noticed he was a sickly blue color. She also saw that Lillian was bleeding profusely. When Rose tried to take the baby from her, Lillian screamed and clutched the baby tightly. She began to hum a lullaby.

Rose helped Anna do what she could to stop the bleeding. When Anna was satisfied that Lillian had been taken care of, she went out side and began to wail and sing in Lakota. She swayed slowly from side to side as she mourned.

Rose, still in shock, knelt on the floor. She pulled her rosary from her pocket and prayed.

After their prayers, the three women huddled together on the floor, rocking and holding the dead little baby. They held each other until Lillian spoke. "Rose, please go get Fr. Logan."

Rose ran up the hill to the small white-frame parsonage and banged on the door.

Fr. Logan jolted from his late-morning nap. He'd been up early for his early Morning Prayer time. He answered the door to see the hysterical Rose Welsley from across the river at his door.

"Fr. Logan!" Rose screamed. "Fr. Logan, come quickly! Lillian has given birth and the baby is not breathing."

Fr. Logan hurried back into the parish house, put a stole around his neck, and ran to the church for a baptismal candle and some holy water. He raced ahead of Rose toward Lillian's home. "Rose, pray to St. Andrew now!" he urged as he passed her by.

Fr. Logan rushed into the kitchen. He took the small bundle from Lillian's arms and felt for a pulse. He said it was too late, and gave the baby to Anna. He told her to prepare it for burial.

Fr. Logan turned and went out of the house. He said he would meet them all at the cemetery in the morning for the burial. Walking back to the parish house, Fr. Logan murmured aloud to himself, "Once again, another soul not prepared for Heaven. Why did the Bishop give me such an assignment? Could I just once have a normal death with all the trimmings? A Latin Requiem Mass with all the fanfare? Do all new priests get locked into such a position, a trial by fire? I am going to have to start a Catechism class. It is time to convert some of these heathen, including that witch doctor, Anna, to the real faith. The Bishop is going to want an accounting for all these unblessed burials and unconverted souls."

The following morning, Lillian, Rose, and Anna walked up the hill toward the cemetery. Lillian and Rose had dressed the little baby in one of the layette pieces they had made, and Anna had tenderly wrapped the little body in a star quilt. There would be no coffin. She handed the little bundle to Lillian to carry. Lillian decided to name him Adam. He was the first male she'd created, and Adam was the first male God had created.

The women looked around the cemetery for Fr. Logan, but he was not within the crude wood fencing. He stood outside the fence and motioned for the women to join him there. He explained Old Joe had offered to dig the grave there outside the fence.

Lillian objected. "Fr. Logan," she said. "I want Adam to be buried next to his father in our family plot. Why has the grave been dug here?"

"Your baby was not baptized," Fr. Logan said. "I cannot bury him in consecrated ground. Only Catholics freed from original and mortal sin can be buried in the consecrated ground of the cemetery. We will start a row here, overlooking the river, for the un-baptized babies from this parish. I am sorry your baby has to be the first. Your baby's soul has gone to Limbo, a place of eternal joy for un-baptized babies, but he will not get to enter the Gates of Heaven nor see the Face of God."

Fr. Logan laid the tiny bundle into the grave, and Lillian fell to the ground in a heap. She held her head in her hands and sobbed. Rose knelt down next to her and tried to console Lillian the best she could. Fr. Logan sprinkled the tiny grave with holy water, and said the words about ashes to ashes and dust to dust. He built a cairn of stones over the grave.

Lillian, racked with sobs, was now angry at God. She glared at Fr. Logan, and pleaded for answers from the young priest.

"What kind of God would not allow this little one to have a proper burial in the cemetery or to be in Heaven with the angels? What kind of God would take my young husband? What kind of God would leave me alone?"

The stoic Fr. Logan had no answers for the grieving young woman. Did he dare say to her at this time, her mortal sins were the cause of all this? Finally moved to say something, he answered, "God has His reasons," he said. "Only the angels and saints know."

Once again, Anna began her sad Lakota song of mourning, and then turned to the three and shared wisdom passed down from her elders. "And so you do not forget," she said, "every dawn as it comes is a holy event, and every day is holy, for the light comes from Wakan Tanka."

"And you," she said, glaring at Fr. Logan, "you must remember that the two-leggeds and all other peoples who stand upon this earth are sacred and should be treated as such!"

The Stranger
1911

Rose's stay with Lillian ended late that summer, and Chris was happy to have his daughter back home. It appeared Rose was satisfied that Lillian was ready to be on her own. Rose had started school in Bismarck that fall.

Chris agreed to school, but not wholeheartedly. He knew that Rose would enjoy her year at school, but he looked forward to having her return home to help on the farm during spring planting. She claimed she liked living in the city, but that her heart was really only at peace out on the quiet prairie.

As Rose relaxed on the porch one evening and admired the pastel pinks and blues of a North Dakota sunset, a young man rode into the yard on a horse. He jumped off the horse spryly, and said, "Evening, Miss. Is the owner of this farm around?"

Just as he asked, Chris stepped out the front door of the house. He never let too many young men be around his daughter alone.

"What can I do for you?" Chris inquired, sizing up the stranger.

"Good evening, sir," the man answered. "My name is Ben Hofts. I am looking for work as a farmhand. I don't expect much in wages, maybe just room and board, but I can plow a field and I'm handy with livestock. I would be happy sleeping in the barn. Do you need such a fella as I?"

Chris eyed the young man. He'd recently been looking for such a farmhand. In fact, he'd been looking for someone suitable for young Rose, too.

"Well, Ben. I am looking for someone to work on the farm, actually. What have you done in the past, and where do you come from? It's not very often anymore that a young fella wants to stay out here on the prairie. Most want to head straight down to South Dakota to the mines and find their fortunes."

Coincidentally, Chris had just been thinking about Rose and how she was getting up there in age. She was almost eighteen now, and most of the young men around here that age, those who would make a decent farmer, had already married. Dependable young men were few and far between in these parts, especially the kind who wanted to farm. Chris yearned to slow down a bit himself, and Mary was still battling those "women's problems," as the doctor said last summer. She wasn't as much help around the farm as she used to be.

"Well Sir, and Miss," Ben said in his southern accent. "I come from Bismarck. I've been working on the railroad, and I originally come from Virginia. I don't like city life; I grew up on a farm, and I want to get back to the good life. I'm lookin' to buy my own piece of land someday, to settle down and raise up some boys of my own."

Chris liked what he was hearing. He didn't know if he could trust a Southerner, but the war was long over.

Anton, Rose's younger brother, sauntered around the corner of the house. The two young men stared at each other as if there were some fleeting moment of recognition. Sizing Ben up, Anton chimed in on the conversation, "Now, who do we have here?"

"Anton, this here is Mr. Ben Hofts, our new farmhand," Chris said. "Take him down to the barn and show him where he can bunk in the hayloft."

Anton threw his father a quick look that said he didn't totally approve, but he knew better than to disobey the old man's orders.

Chris sat down on the big wooden chair on the porch, and he watched Anton lead Ben and his horse down toward the barn. The future of the farm seemed to be continually on his mind. Anton, his only son, really should be the heir to the farm, but he wanted to leave it to Rose. He knew Anton would be furious over such an arrangement, and so he never discussed it. Anton was fickle. What if he decides to take off again like he did just last year? As soon as the spring thaw hit the river and the steamboats were able to travel, Anton took off to Deadwood for whatever reason. A month later, he came back wanting to move back home. That story about having an accident while mining for gold seemed a little contrived somehow. Those bruises Anton sported on his face and that shiner on his eye looked more like he'd gotten his hot-headed self into some kind of brawl. But Chris remembered the story in the Good Book about the prodigal son and he'd decided to let his wayfaring son come back home. There was no killing the fatted calf to celebrate, however, just a few extra chores assigned to keep Anton apprised of where his place is. Chris figured if Rose was in charge of the farm, at least he could control how things were done when he was old and unable to work. Yes, he thought to himself, I sure could use a farmhand.

Chris stood up and held his aching back. He wandered down to the barn, where Anton was showing Ben where he could sleep in the hayloft. He chuckled to himself as he overheard Anton's attempt to be the foreman. "Mr. Hofts, the day starts around here at sunrise," Anton said. "We start with breakfast up at the house, followed by rosary led by my mother, Mary. Tomorrow's work includes moving cattle down to the southern part of the farm."

Ben replied, "Yes, sir, Mr. Welsley. I'll be up before the sun comes up, and I'll be looking forward to breakfast with y'all. Now, if you don't mind, I'd really like to hit the hay early."

Chris almost laughed out loud, thinking, When had Anton ever showed up for morning breakfast at sunrise, let alone rosary? If Mary wouldn't swoon all over him, and get him a late breakfast every day, he might show up on time.

Chris also liked the young man's politeness. He could already tell young Ben had a sense of humor.

Observant as always, Chris noticed that early morning may come far too quickly for Ben. He watched his new farmhand from the house window in the early morning light. Ben ambled out of the barn and made his way toward the water trough, and Chris saw a curse word form on Ben's lips as he did a quick wash-up. Chris stepped away from the window as Ben hurried up the slight hill to the house. He noticed Ben patiently wait on the porch for an invitation to enter.

Chris pondered what Ben may have thought of Rose when they first met on the porch the night before. Ben's eyes had explored his daughter. Is that what is called "Southern Charm"? He made a mental note to watch over her more protectively until he knew this stranger better.

Except for Anton, the Welsley family was all present for an early breakfast the following morning. Mary and Rose busily prepared hotcakes and coffee for Chris, Ben, and a couple of Indians who helped out over the summer months.

As soon as breakfast was over, Mary led the group in the rosary. Chris didn't look pleased when Ben didn't pull out a strand of rosary beads from his pocket. Well, here is the first obstacle, Chris thought. I bet that southern boy isn't Catholic. He's probably Baptist or something. Well, that is changeable. I won't worry about that now.

Chris glared angrily at Anton when he arrived late. As soon as Mary finished the final prayer, she ran to Anton's side. "Anton, you worked too hard yesterday," she crooned. "What can your Mama make you special for breakfast this morning? Did you get enough sleep?" She smoothed down a wayward curl from his forehead.

After the breakfast dishes were done, and the farmyard chores were finished, Rose and Mary spent the remainder of the morning preparing for noon lunch and tending to outside chores. They gathered eggs and fresh beans from the garden, and at noon, Chris, Anton, and Ben happily chewed down cold pork chop sandwiches and cooked beans with bacon before going back off to the field. The women spent the rest of the afternoon with more household chores, and they prepared the evening meal. They worked on mountains of laundry, and they chatted about the new wash machine they planned to purchase in the fall after the crops were sold. Both women were tired of scrubbing clothes on a washboard in a galvanized steel tub.

Rose never knew how to react when Mary became irrational. She claimed her wild mood swings were a result of her "change." Sometimes, Mary acted bizarre, and became so angry about some small detail not going right. She might throw a dish and smash it to bits. Other days, after breakfast and the rosary, she spent the entire day in her room in the dark.

After finishing chores, Rose felt the need to escape from the endless cooking, cleaning, and laundry, plus her mother's incorrigible behavior. She walked down to the river's edge and found her secret sanctuary: Past the pasture and down the hill from the Welsley farmstead was a small inlet of the river that created a quiet pool surrounded by cottonwood trees and bullberry bushes. There in the thicket were different kinds of plants, and one plant to avoid, Rose had learned, was poison ivy.

As Rose wandered across a meadow and down the hill toward the river, she thought about Lillian and Anna. Her friends were starting a business gathering native plants and selling them as medications. They were going to create a compound of herbs and other native plants to help Mama. She wondered if the concoction might be made from some of the same plants that grew in her secret place. The doctor in Bismarck said surgery, a hysterectomy, was going to be the only treatment for Mama, and Rose was certain it was called that because of Mama's hysterical actions. She prayed that the medicines

Anna and Lillian would create might help, instead. Rose had never seen another person in her secret place, and in summertime, when the water was warm enough, she liked to do her bathing here instead of drawing water at the house. The inlet was so well-hidden she felt comfortable stripping down and swimming. As she swam, she sang the lovely Lakota song Anna had taught her about her name.

> *Place a crimson rose in a maiden's hair,*
> *the color of sunrise, on her wedding day fair.*
> *Only a rose carries the fragrance of love,*
> *beckoning her Brave, sent from above.*
> *La, tra, ra la, ra lu…*

Her beautiful soprano voice softly echoed throughout the inlet. The river level was low this time of year and created a warm sandy beach. Today, she would allow herself the luxury of a sun bath.

Because she was fair-skinned, she limited her time, and reluctantly stood up. She brushed the sand from her body, picked up her satchel of clean clothes and homemade soap, and walked slowly to the water's edge. She enjoyed the feeling of sand between bare toes.

Rose stepped into the water and found pleasure as the warm water lapped her skin. Attuned to the familiar sounds in the inlet, Rose was startled by a strange sound.

"Who's there?" she asked, and ran to the beach for her clothes and satchel.

Silence.

She picked up her satchel and ran quickly to a small growth of bushes. Once again, she asked, "Is someone there?"

She had a very strange feeling of being watched.

Rose tried to brush off the feeling. She decided it was probably just a curious deer. Papa had warned her to be on guard, however, because a wolf or mountain lion had been spotted along the river in search of water. She ran quickly back to the house and still shook from fright. Proper rest escaped her that night, but it wasn't the scare during her bath that caused her to be restless. Instead, she anticipated Sunday's activities, and a chance to get to know Ben.

Sunday Service
1911

After finishing morning chores, Ben rambled up the hill toward the Welsley home in pursuit of a hot breakfast and a chance to watch Rose work around the kitchen. It had been a long time since he'd done farm work, and all his muscles ached.

From what Ben had gathered from the other farmhands, Chris Welsley was a strict disciplinarian with his family when it came to church attendance. At the breakfast table, Ben listened quietly as Chris planned the drive into Bismarck for Mass at St. Mary's. The farmer tackled a hearty breakfast of flapjacks and sausages, and between bites, he talked about when they would leave for Bismarck and what needed to be done before they left. The Indians, who bunked with Ben in the barn, told him how in winter, when the river was frozen hard enough, the family would cross over to St. Giles for Mass at the church there, but in summer, the "boss," as they called Chris, liked to drive to Bismarck.

"Ben, the family is going into Bismarck for Mass," Chris announced after breakfast. "Would you want to ride along? I don't know what kind of church you belong to, but you're invited along with our family to Bismarck this morning."

The invitation sounded a little more like a strong recommendation than a polite offer. Feeling as though it would be prudent to attend with the family, Ben agreed. "Well, Mr. Welsley, I am honored you asked me," he said. "Just nudge me if I make a wrong move. I don't really have any church background, but I'm willing to learn."

Ben's answer appeared to have pleased Chris. He felt the farmer's hand on his back, moving him toward the stairs leading to the second floor of the house. "Well, then, come along," Chris said. "You can borrow a suit from Anton. You look about the same size."

Ben noticed the scowl on Anton's face. "Take Ben up to your room and get him cleaned up," Chris ordered. "And yes, you are going along, too."

Anton nodded to Ben. "Follow me," he said. "Let's get you suited up so we can get this over with."

As Ben changed clothes, he felt Anton's eyes following his every move. He noticed Anton staring at the blond hair on his chest. Anton's nose flared when he bent down near to Ben's discarded pile of work clothes, and it appeared to Ben that Anton noticed more than regular farm smells from his clothes. He saw the look of recognition on Anton's face. Clearly, Anton recognized the smell of moonshine.

"Well, Ben, you clean up pretty good!" Anton said.

Ben felt increasingly uncomfortable as Anton eyed him. Was it possible that Anton may recognize him?

Ben felt Anton sizing him up as they descended the stairs. Ben Hofts was the farthest thing from a church-going man. He had come to the farm with plans to be a lot more than just a farmhand. Walking toward the shined-up Model T parked at the front gate, Ben contemplated his real reason for attending Sunday services. Portraying himself a gentleman to the ladies, he offered his hand to Rose and Mary as they stepped into the back seat of the Model T. Chris moved into the driver's side as Anton jumped into the front seat passenger side. Ben stood back, considering where he should sit, when Anton yelled, "Ben, crank 'er up!" and so Ben moved to the front of the car to do the strenuous job of starting the engine. He heard Chris scold Anton.

"Now, just a minute, Anton. Ben is our Sunday guest today. He was gentleman enough to help your Mama and Rose into the car. You can give up your seat today and allow our guest to ride in the front, but open up the rumble. Mama wouldn't be happy if you tried to sit in back with her and Rose and their newly pressed skirts."

"Ben, hop in," Chris called out. "Anton can get the crank."

Anton glowered at Ben as they passed one another on the passenger side of the auto. Ben decided it would be best to watch his back around this one.

As the Sunday travelers started down the road, the conversation turned to the weather, the neighbors, and Bismarck. It appeared to Ben that Chris believed in leaving work and the talk of it behind on Sunday. While the family made small talk, Ben used the time to observe his surroundings. He looked at the road, and the other farms, but he struggled to keep his eyes off Rose. She was dressed in her Sunday finery, and was unbelievably beautiful, and although thinking about Rose was pleasant, Ben decided it would be best to think about business.

Ben needed to move his lucrative moonshine operation to a secluded area near to the farm. His whiskey was popular, so popular that he couldn't keep up with demand with the small still he had hidden just outside of Bismarck. After far too many close calls with revenuers, he decided he should run his operation at night somewhere deep in the countryside.

Growing up in Virginia on a farm and helping with his old man's moonshine operation had given Ben the perfect education, not only to raise the corn he needed, but to make that corn into a nice distillation of white lightning. He not only needed a secluded place down by the river for the still, he needed access to a nice crop of corn growing right next to it.

Ben could not believe his good fortune when he rode into the farm that lucky evening and saw such a beauty sitting on the porch. When the old man came out and hired him on the spot, he believed lady luck was truly on his side. All he had to do now was use his charm, like he did to win over so many of the "ladies" in Bismarck. With luck, he'd soon have a big farm to run his moonshine operation.

Seeing Rose on the porch was a bonus. If he played his cards right, he might be able to call the place his own. The old man obviously had Rose picked out to inherit the place. He could already feel the tension between the old man and his boy. Anton talked big about running the place someday and about the changes he was going to make, but it just wasn't gonna happen as far as Ben could tell. He prided himself on his ability to quickly figure out human nature, and, yes, Rose would make an upstanding wife with all her schooling and such. No one would suspect anything was amiss.

Rose appeared to be a little on the prudish side, but after watching her in the old swimming hole, Ben discovered that she is one mighty fine female specimen. He smiled as he thought about the scene from the evening before, and he was so lost in thought that he nearly said aloud, "And if I can't get her trained to my liking, well, there's sweet Sally in town who's always willing." Now I just have to pretend to be a good boy, he thought. The stars had all aligned, to be sure. Yes, indeed, that old swimming hole is just the place for the still, and the view isn't too shabby, either.

Ben was jostled out of deep thought as the Tin Lizzie's hard, wooden right-front wheel went over a large rock. He had to place his hand over his mouth to stop the string of curse words that nearly rolled out.

"Ben, I am sure you are tired of all this small talk," Rose said from the back seat. "Tell us about yourself."

"Aw, there isn't much to tell, Miss," Ben said. "I grew up on a farm out in Virginia, and never went to much school. I always had to work on the farm. I got no family out there anymore, so came west to work on the railroad. I got tired of that and wanted to get back to farming. Nothin' excitin' like you, going to school and such."

"C'mon, Ben," Anton commented from the rumble seat. "I bet you got a little more than that to tell."

Ben bristled. He turned to face Anton, and the moment of recognition came to him. "Nope," Ben said. "I've lived a pretty straight life. Hard work and day-to-day, that's pretty much it." He faced forward again and realized how he knew Anton, and panicked for a moment. *Oh, yes, he thought. I've seen that slithering snake around Bismarck. That boy has a penchant for gambling, and I just saw him behind the closed doors of a couple of my customer's blind pig operations a few weeks ago. He's gonna be nothing but trouble for me. I'll have to use sage root to keep my hair and mustache dyed black, but I can't do it everywhere all the time. Hell, I saw Anton staring me up and down getting dressed this morning. It's just a matter of time before he figures out where he saw me before.*

"No, Anton, I'm sure my life is nuthin' like your gentleman's life."

The family finally arrived in front of a large church with tall spires, a very impressive sight. Only recently built, the church had already acquired a notable history: The stained glass windows were said to have been donated by mostly women, and one window had been donated by the Marquise Medora von Hoffman in her husband's memory.

During the seemingly endless church service, Ben excused himself, and said he needed some air. High Mass was known to last well over an hour, so he figured he had time to check on some orders. He'd done some of his best business during that time, when most local lawmen were at Mass. The main hub of his business was just a short walk from the church, and if he got business taken care of quickly, he'd have time for a little pleasure.

Ben hurried over to the large hotel under construction on Main Street. He made his way into the basement and found an opening to the tunnel network below the new brick-and-mortar buildings on the street. On a couple of the doors, he gave the secret knock. As Ben's patrons cracked open the doors, he made small talk, collected their orders, and exchanged cash. These were the customers he liked best; they ran their own secret operations, usually involving ladies, gambling, and alcohol. They were his pay-up-front customers, and they had come to trust him, but he feared their retribution should he not deliver.

With a bounty of pre-delivery payments in his pockets, Ben knocked on a door that emanated cheap perfume. He found Sally "unemployed," as most of her customers were at church services. Ben enjoyed his animated, short "visit" with his favorite soiled dove.

Happily immoral and corrupt, Ben was able to get back into the family pew before Benediction ended. Yes, thought Ben, this is going to be just dandy. It's only August, so I have plenty of time to get a shack built and the still set up before winter. I just wonder how long it will take before I walk down this aisle at St. Mary's as a respectable groom.

Sleepless Nights
1911

The drive back to the farm after Mass in Bismarck was quite merry. The family sang many of their favorite hymns to pass the time. After they drove into the farmstead, Ben remained at the auto to talk with Papa, and Rose overheard Ben ask her father if he could begin courting her. She'd just met Ben, and she knew so little about him, so she was even more surprised when Papa said, "Yes," and offered Ben the use of the Model T, Papa's pride and joy, and which represented the culmination of much hard work.

Weeks before, Rose and Anton had been invited to a neighbor's home for a sing-along, followed by supper. Now, Papa suggested Rose invite Ben along, and she suspected Papa was using the invitation as an event to get the courtship started.

When the Saturday night of the sing-along came around, Rose observed Papa as he nervously watched Ben start his beloved car. She smiled as Ben expertly drove to the front door to pick her up, and Anton begrudgingly jumped into the rear seat. He sent a look at Ben to communicate his disdain. As they made a turn to the south toward the Muester farm, Rose turned back to see Papa waving. Chris watched until they drove out of sight.

The Muester farm had a thick, cottonwood-tree-lined gravel road that led to an impressive white house. Like the Welsley's, the Muester farmhouse had a decorative large porch that stretched around the front. Rose entered the large parlor on Ben's arm and blushed at the whispers and stares they received. The Muester's son, Rueben, stared at the couple and you could almost hear his heart hit the floor. In fact, he immediately excused himself and was not seen the rest of the evening.

Mrs. Muester played the piano beautifully, and all of the guests had a wonderful time singing. Afterward, they shared a large meal.

Rose thought it was nice to see the family again. She'd gone to school with the Muester children, but never mingled very much with them socially. Because the Muesters weren't Catholic, in Papa's eyes they weren't quite acceptable, but there were so few young people for Rose and Anton to socialize with, the families met on occasion despite their differences.

The Muester and Welsley children attended the same one-room country school. Rueben was a couple years older than Rose, and she recalled how he'd taken a strong liking to her. He'd continually follow her about and pass her little notes, and one day, she saw a large heart with an arrow through it etched out on a large tree trunk near the school. Inside the heart were the words "Rose and Rueben Forever." Rueben was brazen enough to ask Papa if he could call on her, and Papa said absolutely not.

Rose listened to the lovely singing. She enjoyed hymns of all kinds, but if Papa knew that some of the songs performed around the piano that night were not Catholic hymns, he wouldn't want her to sing along. The beautiful words didn't seem in any way contradictory to what she believed, and she marveled at their spiritual message.

Ben spent his time visiting with Arthur Muester, Rueben's father. Rose was happy Ben had found someone to converse with. In fact, Rose thought they seemed to hit it off very well for strangers who'd never met before.

Later in the evening, after assisting with kitchen clean-up, a very exhausted Rose looked for Rueben to thank him for the evening. It was time to say goodnight to the Muester family and to the other guests before they left the gathering. Meanwhile, Ben searched the yard for Anton, but he was nowhere to be found. After checking with the other guests, Rose and Ben discovered Anton had slipped off toward Linton and to a popular pool hall there along with some other young men. As she asked if others knew where Rueben was, Rose felt a distant feeling of annoyance coming from Ben. She shrugged the cold feeling away. Why would he be upset? she thought.

With the moon shining overhead, and the stars twinkling in the large expanse of the North Dakota sky, Ben drove Rose to the front porch and helped her out of the auto. Seeing no light on in the house, Ben walked Rose to the front door, and then stored the "T" in the shed. Rose waited for Ben on the porch to say goodnight. She watched Ben's masculine moves as he climbed the steps toward her. Rose felt warmth creep into her cheeks when Ben spoke. "Rose," he whispered, "you look lovely in the moonlight. I look forward to seeing you in the morning at breakfast."

Rose looked toward the moon. "Tomorrow is Sunday," she said, "and we will all be going to church. Will you join us?"

"Only if you let me sit next to you this time," he said. "By the way, what was the problem with that Muester fellow?"

"You mean Rueben?" she asked. "When we were in school, he always wanted to be my sweetheart. It was just puppy love, nothing else."

Ben seemed annoyed. He took both of Rose's hands in his and held them tight, a little too tight for Rose's liking. He said, "Rose, I am going to court you very seriously. I don't want you looking at other fellas. Tell me you won't." He released Rose's hands. "Good night, Rose," he said. "It was a pleasurable evening," and he gave her a quick kiss on the cheek.

Holding her cheek where Ben kissed her, Rose looked into transparent blue eyes. "Ben," she said, "I will give you a fair chance, but I'm not promising anything. I know Papa likes you, and he wants me to marry someone who can help him here on the farm, but I have plans. I want to finish school and, someday, to teach in Bismarck. You know that schoolteachers aren't allowed to be seen with a beau."

Rose walked into the house and gently shut the door behind her. She leaned against the door, and held the soft kiss Ben had placed on her cheek. She walked toward the staircase, unpinned her hair, and shook it loose as she ascended the steps toward her bedroom. Her heart pounded from being so close to Ben. She slipped silently into her room and undressed in the dark. Lately, she had avoided dressing and undressing with the lamp on because she had a strange feeling that she was being watched. It wasn't because Ben was living in the barn, she told herself, because the feeling had actually started before he came to live at the farm. She brushed the thought aside and climbed under her quilt. The late summer, North Dakota evening was very cool, and as she lay watching clouds pass over the moon outside her window, she began to think about Rueben. My, how tall and handsome he'd become! She'd heard he was quite a businessman, and she'd also heard he was planning to purchase the mercantile in St. Giles, and to open a grain elevator near the railroad station. Her mind drifted to her friend across the river. I wonder if Lillian knows about what Rueben is planning, she thought. I should visit Lillian soon. Her thoughts turned to the kind of man she would want to marry someday. She admitted she is attracted by Ben's dark hair, his blue eyes, and rough manners, but she'd always thought of settling down with a more intellectual man. A man with an education, perhaps another teacher, someone, well, like Rueben.

"Oh, drat!" she whispered aloud. She rose up, wandered to her window, and opened it for a little fresh air. Was it her imagination, or did someone just run down the hill toward her secret hideaway? It'd be best to get some sleep. Her mind was beginning to play tricks on her. Everyone in their right mind would be in bed, because Papa's call for everyone to rise for breakfast and church would come far too soon. What was the strange noise she sometimes heard at night? It sounded as though there were mice between the walls.

The Picnic
1911

Early Sunday morning, a sleepy Ben made a point of sitting next to Rose on the ride to Bismarck. The smell of homemade soap evoked images of Rose sunbathing without a stitch on in her hideaway. Ben allowed himself to imagine what it would be like the first time he showed her the ways of love.

During Mass, Ben figured he better not run off on his visits to Sally or his customers. The night before, he managed to convince Old Joe to ferry some southern comfort across to one of his partners, who waited for it across the river. Ben recognized that Old Joe was going to become very useful, because all he wanted in pay was a pint now and then. Ben felt the weight of the silver in his pockets, and he enjoyed the sound of silver dollars jingling as he walked. Yes, this morning he could afford to put off business for a day or two. He deemed it necessary to start using his charms on Rose.

Last night, he'd noticed her reaction to his kiss, and although she acted all proper, he knew women well enough to know that every one of them will eventually succumb to natural instinct, especially with a man like himself. During the drive back from church, Ben asked Chris if Rose could go for a Sunday afternoon picnic with him. Chris gave his blessing, so the couple returned to the house and packed a picnic lunch of country fried chicken, homemade buns, and preserves.

Ben followed as Rose led the way through the meadow. He was enticed by her hips' hypnotic sway as she showed him a favorite family picnic spot. Finding a large tree for shade, they spread out a horse-hair blanket and sat down to eat. Ben quickly grabbed a chicken leg from the wicker picnic basket, but Rose stopped his hand. Getting the wrong idea, he pulled Rose to him and tried to kiss her and with more passion this time, but Rose slapped him hard on the cheek and cried out, "Ben, what are you trying to do? We must say grace before eating."

Ben apologized. They finished their meal without speaking.

After lunch, Ben lay back and closed his eyes. He began to strate-gize the best way to seduce Rose. All his experience with women up to now was with willing women of the expensive kind. He'd never called on a proper woman, or spent time socially with one. He covered his face with his hat, but he watched Rose out of the corner of his eye as she tidied up after lunch. She'd bowed her head and said a prayer after the meal. He observed her movements as she cleaned up, and he must have dozed off until he heard her speak. "Ben, are you awake?" Rose asked. "Ben, would you like to walk around the farm and get to know where all of Papa's pastures and fields are?"

"Rose, there is nothing else I would rather do," Ben lied.

As they walked through the pastures and around planted fields, she showed him the wild trees from which she picked berries to use in preserves. Ben made a mental note of the best spots to hide his still. Remembering his manners, he took Rose by the arm as they walked. They paused to watch pheasants in the deep grass, and when out of eyesight from the house, Ben turned toward Rose, and he pulled her near. This time Rose did not resist, and she gave in to the kiss and to the embrace from Ben. When he tried for another, she pushed him away, and told him to walk her home. He'd felt her young heart pound-ing hard for that instant when his chest was against hers. He would patiently give her time to adjust to her new feelings. He assessed the moment within himself and surmised that the embrace and the kiss weren't bad for a start. She simply needs help to relax, he thought, and he knew just how to help her do that.

Harvest Time
1911

Harvest time was the busiest time of the year on the farm. The crops had to be mowed down and bundled for threshing. Everyone, including the women, was expected to be in the field from sunrise to sunset bundling wheat stalks to form triangular piles called shocks. The work was back-breaking in the ninety-plus-degree heat, and Ben grimaced as he held a bundle under each arm. He set them down firmly with a grunt and swore as he reached for two more. He dropped them when he swatted yet another mosquito, and so he sat on a field rock to scratch the many bites that had inflamed on his neck. He looked toward the endless oat pasture, and it made him all the more determined to make sure that his liquor business would succeed.

After the field was ready, they drove teams of horses with wagons into the field. Up and down the rows, able hands used pitchforks to throw bundles into the carts, which were then taken to the threshing machine, where the bundles were thrown in to separate wheat from chaff. They loaded the grain back into the wagons and then took it to storage for future sale. A huge number of laborers were required to finish one field.

Early one Saturday morning at breakfast, Ben listened closely as Chris explained the work ahead. "Wouldn't you know it; the oats are just about dry, and tomorrow would be ideal for threshing, but tomorrow's Sunday, and even if I got permission from the priest to work, I doubt I would get any help." Chris took the opportunity to give Ben a quick lesson about the subject of work on a Sunday. Ben picked at his oatmeal. Chris went on. "If the farmer wants to work on Sunday, because it is necessary," he said, "he needs to get permission to do so from the priest. Working on a Sunday is considered a mortal sin, and no Catholic farmer wants to chance committing a damning sin during such a dangerous time of year. Farm accidents happen far too often."

Ben's ears perked up at the sound of accident; he was always interested in a new "fatal" accident idea. "So what kind of accident can happen out in a field full of shocks?" he asked. "They look pretty harmless to me."

"Well, a couple years ago," Chris said, "there was a young fella up on the threshing machine, and something wasn't quite right with him, but he was a hard worker. Some of the other boys liked to tease the poor soul, so when he was on top of the threshing machine and pitching shocks into the feeder for grinding, some fool threw a bull snake at him. I never saw who did it, exactly, but Anton was in the bunch, and he wouldn't tell me who the guilty party was. I've never seen a rattlesnake on this side of the river, but those bull snakes look just about like them from a distance. Anyway, that boy lost his balance, and he fell into the feeder. Needless to say, it was horrible. We got him pulled out, but by the time we did, he was a goner. You know, I've never seen some of them other boys since, and I was hoping Anton would've tattled so that we could've gotten the law involved, but none of the other men wanted to get the sheriff. They said that boy had a tough life, and he was probably in a better place, anyway. It sounded to me like some of the others didn't want their boys in trouble. I'm sure God will punish whoever did it by making them burn in Hell for eternity." On the way to the field, Ben visualized Anton up on that feeder. He'd had about enough of this back-breaking work. It couldn't be over soon enough.

When harvest was nearly finished, the locals had reason to celebrate, and there was more money to be spent on alcohol, so Ben enjoyed large profits from his bootleg business. He continued to court Rose, and he could tell that she was relaxing and enjoying his attention. He brought her gifts whenever he returned from one of his "business trips" to Bismarck, and he needed an excuse to go to Bismarck each week. He told Chris that he wanted to finish his Catechism studies so that he could be confirmed. Duped by Ben's sincerity, Chris encouraged the trips into the city, especially when Ben mentioned his intention to be a good Catholic son-in-law and to be baptized because he wanted to be ready to ask for Rose's hand in marriage very soon.

To avoid bad reports, Ben would meet with the priest, but then the rest of the night he would make his deliveries and spend some time with Sally. Business continued to boom at the "blind pigs," the name given to legitimate businesses that doubled as liquor establishments in secret.

During one trip to Bismarck, Ben noticed Rueben Muester going into the lumber store. He decided it was time to make his intentions clear to Rueben. "Rueben, I want to have a few words with you," Ben said from across the muddy street. "I know that you have had an interest in Rose, but I want to let you know that she has agreed to marry me."

Rueben stopped in his tracks and turned to face Ben. "Ben, isn't it?" He stood an arm's length away. "I actually visited with Rose myself just two days ago," he said. "I saw her out walking toward the river and we had a short conversation. She didn't say anything about marriage. She said she was planning to move to Bismarck to secure a teaching position. And for your information, I plan to call on her then, when she's out of reach from her overly protective father." With that, Rueben turned to walk away.

Ben bristled. He spun Rueben around and grabbed him by the throat. "You stay away from her, do you hear?" he barked. "If you don't, I'll be happy to share some very good information I have about your old man. I know he's planning to run for Governor. I also know that he has a taste for a certain brew and for an old gal named Sally."

Rueben pushed Ben's hand away, and spewed, "I don't know what you're talking about. My father is a highly respected member of his church and of the Masonic lodge. Get the hell out of my way."

The following morning at breakfast, after everyone had left the kitchen for morning chores, Ben grabbed Rose by the arm and led her roughly into the summer kitchen pantry. He held her arms tightly until she started to cry. "Don't you ever go near that Rueben," he warned. "I don't want to hear that you were sneaking off to talk to him, do you understand?"

A Visit to Lillian
Fall 1911

Rose hurried to her bedroom. She threw herself down on the bed and cried into her crossed arms. She felt trapped and decided what she really needed was to visit her friend, Lillian.

On Friday, Rose received permission from Papa to go to St. Giles for the weekend. She skipped down to the beach to where Old Joe met travelers who wished to cross to the west side of the river. She paid Joe the fare, ten cents, and sat on the raft as he maneuvered through the fast current. On the other side, she stepped gingerly onto shore and looked for the path through the tall weeds that led up the side of the riverbank.

As she grasped for a branch to pull herself up the last steep, dirt step, she saw Lillian. The friends embraced and giggled as they looked each other over. Rose was surprised by Lillian's physical changes. She'd lost her roundness and looked wonderfully slim and trim. She'd begun to style her hair in the latest fashion, too, by parting it on the side. Her tresses fell in waves to frame her face, and her complexion was clear. She had pierced ears. "Lillian, you look wonderful!" Rose chirped. "You're like a butterfly that has come out of its cocoon, and you're glowing, like you're in…" Rose stopped before she said the word "love."

"Rose, it's alright," Lillian answered. "Actually, I do have much to tell you, but let's wait until we're comfortable." They kept their arms around each other during the short walk into St. Giles, but before they reached Lillian's home, they paid a visit to little Adam's grave. They also opened the wooden gate and walked inside the cemetery to stand quietly before Josef's grave.

That evening, the young ladies dined together at the little restaurant where Lillian worked. They talked late into the night, and their conversation turned to young men. At first, Rose found the conversation uncomfortable, because it didn't seem like the proper amount of mourning time had passed for Lillian to have such a discussion, but then she realized it had been over a year since Josef died. How could she not have seen Lillian in over a year? And then she remembered school, Mama, Ben, and the farm.

Lillian jarred her from her thoughts. "Rose, tell me all about Ben," she said. "You wrote in your letter that you think he plans to ask you to marry him. I am so happy for you!"

"Lillian, I'm so confused. I don't think I'm ready for that. You know I want to teach, but Papa is the one who seems ready for me to be married. He keeps saying that he wants to slow down, and he and Anton fight constantly about how things are supposed to get done around the farm. Anton threatens to leave and get his own farm, or to go back to the mines, and I feel guilty, like I should just give up on the idea of teaching to be sure the farm is run properly for Papa. And Mama is always sickly. She continues to have bouts of women problems like she did when I saw you in Bismarck last year. That's why I had to get away, to leave my problems on the other side of the river for a few days. Ben was so upset. I wouldn't be surprised if he shows up here."

"I hope he does," Lillian said. "I want to meet him. He'll have to meet with my approval." Rose noticed how Lillian's voice crooned. "Rose," she continued. "I have a new beau, too. He says he knows you. He just moved into town and purchased the mercantile. You know, I've been working there since Josef's accident. He added a small bungalow to the rear of the store to live in for the time being, and he's planning to build an elevator across the road next to the railroad depot. He's very handsome. He told me his parents had lived down the road from you, but recently sold their farmstead and moved into Bismarck. Mr. Muester is planning to run for Governor, and Mrs. Muester is also very well-known in social circles. Do you know Rueben Muester?"

Rose nearly reeled backward in shock. Lillian took in her strange reaction.

Lillian cried, "Rose, what is it?"

Rose composed herself. She said softly, "Yes, I know Rueben. I went to school with him. What will your parents say? You do know he is a Lutheran, don't you? His parents are high society; do you think they are going to accept a woman who has a history into their family? Do you want another quick marriage in a parlor again?"

Lillian stared at Rose. "Are you quite finished?" she asked. "What's the matter with you? Why are you chiding me like this?" She stood up and moved away from the table.

Feeling guilty, Rose stood to face her friend. "Lillian," she said. "There was a time when Rueben wanted to court me."

Lillian turned away and fidgeted with the ruffle on her blouse. "Rose, will it always be like this?" she asked. "You, the perfect, angel-faced, well-to-do friend—and I, the second-class girl happy to have a friend like you? I really thought our friendship was special." Lillian smoothed the front of her dress. "I feel like my life is starting over with Rueben," she said. "I don't care if we get married in a barn, because I love him, and I want you and me and Ben and Rueben to be friends someday. Can we try?" She pulled back a wavy lock that had fallen in front of her eyes. "I can see if Rueben's influence around Bismarck can find you that teaching job," she said. "He has friends of means."

"I'm sorry, Lillian," Rose answered. She bit her lower lip for a moment. "It was just such a surprise. I wish you well, I really do."

The remainder of the weekend went along much better. Lillian showed off her impressive garden of herbs and flowers, and told Rose about the things she'd learned from Anna. She explained how to make special teas to improve her health, and she mixed up a potion of black cohosh with other herbs for Rose to take back to her mother for her female problems. She explained to Rose how Anna had also helped her spiritually, but Rose questioned Anna's mystical teachings. "Lillian," she said, "you know that some things that Anna has been telling you are probably not what we believe as Catholics. You've always been a very devout Catholic."

"Now, Rose," Lillian answered. "I enjoy hearing about the Great Spirit and the creation story. When I listen to Anna, she makes me feel as though I am a specially created person in the eyes of God. That gives me peace. At church, I've spent many hours talking to Fr. Logan about sin, and it makes me feel that I always need to do something to make sure Josef is not going to suffer in Purgatory, and that there is nothing at all I can do for Adam, that he's forever in Limbo. Fr. Logan said I should make indulgences and have Masses said, but Anna doesn't believe all that. Rose, why do I feel as though God is too complicated and un-accepting?"

"Lillian, I don't know how to answer you," Rose said. "I never question; I just accept what I've been taught. That's the difference between you and me. Sometimes, I wish I were you."

When the women parted Sunday evening, they put all hard feelings behind them and decided that when the river froze over, they would plan to socialize through the holidays. They resolved to do things as couples with their beaus so that the young men could become better-acquainted. They made a promise that their friendship would be eternal.

When Rose stepped onto Old Joe's raft to return home, she waved goodbye and then waited for Old Joe to launch the raft away from the shore. Lillian waved back to her and began gathering berries and flowers along the riverbank, placing them into a basket. Rose watched as Rueben bounded down the trail toward Lillian, but when he reached the water's edge and noticed Rose on the raft, he ignored Lillian and rushed to the riverbank to hand Rose a small package. "Farewell sweets for the sweet," he said, cheerfully.

Lillian dropped her basketful of chokecherry branches and flowers. She turned and sprinted up the riverbank holding her apron to her face, but it was too late for Rose to follow after her; Old Joe had pushed away from shore.

On the east side of the river, Ben was waiting while Rose stepped off the raft onto the sandy riverbank. He leaned against a tree and smelled bad, the smell of alcohol. "Ah, parting is such sweet sorrow, huh, Rose?" he said, and pulled her toward him. He tried to get a kiss from her, but Rose hissed. "Leave me alone, Ben," she said. "I have to think about what I want to do this fall, and it may not include you."

"We'll see about your fall plans," he slurred. "I have plans, too, and they include you."

Rose struggled to push Ben's hands from her waist, but Ben only tightened his grip.

"You're a fighter, huh? Well, I like that in a woman. Go ahead, scream; I like that, too. Who's going to hear you out here?"

Rose escaped his grip and fled up the riverbank toward home, tears in her eyes. She tried to make sense of her life and could hear Ben calling for her. "Rose, I'm sorry. I was missing you so terribly. Please forgive me. I promise to never act this way again."

Anton
Fall 1911

On a bluff only a short distance from the boat landing, Anton watched the confrontation between Ben and Rose. Their relationship wasn't as cordial as it had appeared around the farm. He nearly laughed out loud as he watched Rose throw Ben's hands off her hips, and watched Ben follow her up the side of the riverbank.

I need to get her off to that teaching job in Bismarck, Anton thought. And then, like the good citizen I am, I'll turn in Ben to the revenuers. Yep, I know what kind of sideline he has. When I tell the old man about this, Ben can kiss his big scheme goodbye. I've been watching that still go up down by the river, and I've been watching that good-for-nothing spy on Rose. What do I care? Maybe she will drown herself. A drowning sure has been known to happen in this river before. If that fails, I'll have to think up another plan, maybe a farm accident of some kind. I've worked too hard to let the farm slip out of my hands.

Anton followed the couple at a safe distance, just out of sight. He hated his sister, and his mind fumed over the possibility that he may lose his inheritance. The old man is about to keel over from something, he thought. When it comes to the farm, he's defying all normal reason. I know he plans to leave the place to Rose, and that's why he's all fired up to get her married off to Ben, but he thinks Ben is some upright, Catechism-studying, hardworking future-farmer.

I won't tell the old man about him until spring, he decided. Winter is a tough time to come by extra money for poker, and so a little game of blackmail for a few months might just pay for my winter activities. When spring comes, I'll let the old cat out of the bag. If Ben thinks he can outsmart me, he better put his thinking cap back on. He doesn't know about the day that snoopy sheriff and his deputy showed up with that poster looking for him. He did a good job of cleaning up—shaved the beard, grew the mustache—heck, he even figured out how to dye his hair black, but there was no disguising those baby blue eyes; they're so light they appeared almost clear on that black-and-white poster.

Anton had a weakness, and he knew it. He needed the farm income to support his gambling activities. He'd tried gold mining in South Dakota for a while, but he spent everything he mined, and then some. He'd gambled everything in the casinos, and what he didn't gamble, he used to pay the ladies in the brothels.

Lately, however, things began to change. Anton was sure his gambling skills were now honed enough to get back what he lost. Mining for gold itself was too much hard work; there are easier ways to make big money. He'd created quite a story about his injuries while mining, something to tell the folks when he returned home. Surely, he couldn't tell the old man he was nearly beaten to death over a card game in a saloon. Until he could get back down there to settle the debt, he needed to keep an eye on what was going on up here. The old man would be furious to know that he actually gambled a load of lumber that they needed for an addition to the barn, but Lady Luck had been with him that day: He did win that bet, but had yet to win back the load of grain that he'd lost. He was going to have to do some explaining, or better yet, find some extra cash. Luckily, he knew where Ma kept her "church money" stashed. She'd never suspected it was him who kept "borrowing" from it. She'd always blamed the Indian hired help. She used to blame the boy that Pa had around to help for a while, the not-quite-right boy who worked farm-to-farm at odd jobs. That boy sure was scared of snakes.

Monday morning, when Pa sent Anton and Ben out to finish some final work for the harvest, Anton decided it was time to let Ben know what he suspected. Ben worked at hitching up the team of horses while Anton found a way to avoid the work of lifting the heavy, black yokes. He rested on the bench of the wagon and held the reins, pretending to untangle them. "Ben, I think you're a smart-enough fella, and I think you know, that I know, that you have a little something going on down there by Rose's old swimming hole."

Ben continued working.

"Oh, yeah," Anton said. "I've watched you watching her swim around without a stitch on, and I can tell you like women, maybe more than is necessary. For me, yeah, that trip into Bismarck every so often is plenty enough, but you—you seem to want it both ways. You want an upright stylish woman for a wife, but some rowdy little wench on the side. Don't worry; I don't care what you and Rose are up to, but I do care about what you're pretending to be; that's what's really bothering me."

Ben stepped around from the front of the large draft horse. He looked up at Anton. "Oh, pray tell, what am I pretending?" he asked. "You got a nice-looking woman for a sister, and what's wrong with a little sneak peek now and then? Heck, I saw you looking, too. Talk about pretending; that loving brother act docsn't fool mc. It seems you mean to enjoy some other kind of loving. C'mon on, spit it out. What's really the big problem?"

"You," Anton snarled, "pretending to be a saint of the Catholic Church, but running that moonshine operation down there by the river, that's what's got me. I'm sure you ain't making wine for the altar, either, and did you know that sheriff was out here looking for you? Sounds like you're a big player in the booze-running up there in Bismarck. There's a nice reward out for you."

Ben turned back to the riggings on the horse.

Anton continued. "I suppose you know about that load of grain I lost on a gamble up in Bismarck." he said. "Talk sure flies around town. It seems I'm going to need some greenbacks to cover it with the old man, but I think we can arrange ourselves a little deal. You hand over some of your profits to me, and I'll keep quiet, so you can keep the blind pigs full for the winter."

Ben stopped and turned to look at Anton. He squinted, and his mouth itched to speak.

Anton laughed. "Heck, I'll even help you make sure those profits are coming in," he said. "We could go in partners: You make bootleg, and I keep quiet for cash."

Ben reached up, and with one large hand, he pulled Anton down from the wagon. They faced each other with fists up and then ended up wrestling on the ground. The next thing they knew, each of them was getting a bang on the back of the head with the handle of a pitchfork. Anton, in a rage, screamed at his father. "Get that crook off this farm and away from Rose," he said, "if you know what's good for this family!" He glared at Ben. "I will deal with you later," he hissed. "You know what you need to do. If you don't get the chore I need done before dark, you pack your gear and get out!"

Chris stuck the handle of the pitchfork out to stop Anton's retreat. "I'm the one who's in charge here," Chris said, "and I'll be the one to do the firing and the hiring. Now, shake hands like men, and apologize like Christians. I expect to see you in the house for rosary and penance tonight. Oh, and Anton, you help Ben get his gear rounded up, because I'm having him move out of the hayloft. We'll build him a spare room in the attic of the house for winter."

Anton should have expected the old man's involvement, but he'd become so riled up, he'd forgotten how voices carry around the farm. He should've known that once he got into a shouting match, and then into a fist-fight, the old man would come around to break it up before someone got hurt. It wouldn't have been the first time his old man broke up one of his fights.

Anton had been about ready to pull his farm knife to defend himself before he felt the wooden end of the pitchfork at his temple. Anton never let a score go unsettled; he would settle up with Ben another time.

Lillian and Rueben
Fall 1911

After he found out Rose would probably marry Ben, Rueben decided to give Lillian the chance to be someone significant in his life. Having her for a business partner or a companion would allow him the opportunity to see Rose now and then and, after all, Lillian was Rose's best friend; they were bound to spend time together.

Rueben asked Lillian to join him in Bismarck to see a play at the Orpheum. He arranged for dinner at the Hotel McKenzie with his parents so that Lillian could meet them. Lillian wore a lovely wool suit in the latest fashion, and the periwinkle blue with black trim set off her dark hair. Rueben had just received several new suits from his father and he decided to dress up for the occasion, as well. His dark grey, wool suit with pinstriped vest was perfectly tailored to his tall frame.

Lillian and Rueben rode to Mandan in Rueben's new Lion 40 automobile. Rueben boasted that he'd paid $1,600 for the car, which had four seats and a self-starter. No more cranking! After the twenty-five mile drive to the Missouri River, the couple waited patiently for the ferry to haul the vehicle across from the Mandan side to the Bismarck side. Rueben nervously watched the swift current as they crossed, while Lillian, ever the adventurer, appeared to enjoy the ride immensely.

The evening went well, until dinner. Rueben's mother asked Lillian all kinds of questions about her background, and Rueben watched the conversation closely. He knew Lillian well enough to know that she had one major weakness in her social skills: She had no qualms talking about anything and everything. No subject was taboo, not her personal life, religion, or even politics. When she began to ramble on about Josef and losing the baby, Rueben panicked. He tried to get her attention and to shush her as she began talk about how she'd had a "shotgun" wedding and about all the problems she'd had with her family. After Lillian had finished her entire history, Rueben resisted looking into his mother's face. His parents suddenly excused themselves from the dinner and told Rueben that next time he was in Bismarck, they wanted to see him, alone.

Rueben had two ways of dealing with his problems: One was flight; the other was drawing inward and being silent. Following dinner, Rueben became very quiet, while Lillian annoyed him with her constant banter about his parents, the play, and the dinner. He was so humiliated, he couldn't speak.

Despite the irritating chatter from Lillian, the drive home along the river to St. Giles was beautiful. When Rueben didn't respond to Lillian's babble, the couple drove in silence and gazed at the stars. It was an Indian Summer night, which meant the temperature for fall felt unseasonably warm. The full harvest moon reflected in the waters of the Missouri River, and it seemed to follow the river as they drove toward St. Giles. Rueben couldn't help but think about Rose. Was she looking at the same moon? he wondered. Was she in the arms of that snake, Ben?

He broke his silence, and asked Lillian if they could stop and park for just a little while to enjoy the unusual fall evening. When she agreed, they drove to the top of the hills overlooking the river. As they admired the wide expanse of the sky and the full moon bobbing on the river, Rueben gingerly took Lillian's hand.

"Lillian, I'm sorry," he said. "I'm sorry my mother acted the way she did at dinner. She had no right to ask you all those personal questions. She says she has 'moral' standards and a 'reputation' to uphold, but if she only knew."

"Only knew what?"

"Oh, it's nothing," he said. "It's just some family things. I'd rather not discuss it. What I'd like to do is just sit here and enjoy the view."

Rueben wondered what Lillian would think if she knew that by the view, he meant things across the river like the rooftop of Rose's home. He was able to see the Welsley farmstead from this vantage point.

After some time looking out over the river, Lillian became chilled, and she asked Rueben to take her home. It appeared to her that he was in some kind of deep daydream and totally unaware she was there.

Rueben started the car and drove down the steep hill toward the little town. He walked Lillian to the door of her small house and gave her a light peck on the cheek. Lillian wondered when he was going to make a more amorous move. Maybe it would have to be her move.

After all of her problems last year, Lillian had been happy to begin spending time with her parents again—she believed Chris Welsley had something to do with their willingness to accept her back into the family fold—and so Lillian asked her parents if they'd like to have a meal with her and Rueben. She arranged for dinner at her little house and invited her parents as guests for the first time. She set the table with a lovely lace tablecloth and made their favorite meal of creamed chicken and mashed potatoes, and she thought about how although her parents had shopped at the mercantile, they'd not had the chance to really get to know Rueben. She imagined her parents becoming excited about her new beau, and knew they must be proud of her social status and how she was establishing herself in the community.

All went well until the dinner conversation turned to the one subject that Lillian knew would be best to avoid. Her hope was that once they got to know Rueben, any differences would seem insignificant—after all, it was almost 1912—but the conversation grew cold when Lillian's parents asked Rueben about his religion. When he mentioned he was Lutheran, that was all they needed to know, and dinner grew strained between the couples. The elder Kruenfels made a weak excuse to leave before dessert, and politely said their farewells to Rueben.

Lillian walked them to the door alone, and they gave Lillian a warning as she said her goodbyes: If she decided to marry this young man in his present state, it would be without them.

A year after Josef had died, Lillian's mourning had been over. She'd stopped wearing black dresses and it felt like coming out into the sunshine. During the past year, she'd taken control of her own destiny by staying busy in her home industry. She'd become creative in a new, exciting endeavor that seemed to keep her skills in constant demand. She'd taught herself to create beautiful, delicious confectionary products that grew popular for social occasions, not only in St. Giles, but in the surrounding area. Her sumptuous chocolates were in such high demand that she was required to hire the help of Anna full time to keep up with orders. Anna and Lillian also kept extremely busy making home remedies for everything from constipation to infertility, and during summer and fall, the two women spent many hours on the St. Giles hillside harvesting plants needed for elixirs, teas, and powders, the natural medicines in demand from their many customers. Lillian liked to hear Anna talk about the medicines as if they had lives of their own, and she knew Anna believed that if you didn't have faith in the spiritual side of medicine, it wouldn't be "good medicine." When doctors failed to heal their woes, many came to Anna, who told Lillian that there was a cure on the prairies and hillsides for almost every disease, if you knew the proper mixture.

Rueben felt the first profits of his successful business operations in St. Giles. The mercantile became the first in the area to sell gasoline, and more and more automobiles were beginning to appear, as owning an auto was becoming more of a necessity than a luxury.

Rueben's financial backing was, in most, his father's friends. Using their investments in his business ventures, he built a grain elevator and scale in St. Giles, which would allow the local farmers to weigh and store their grain in St. Giles, and either ship it north to Bismarck, or ship it south by rail. The process saved the local farmers time and money.

Rueben was a gifted businessman and an excellent salesman, and he clearly understood that he was being groomed by his father and his investors to enter politics in the very near future.

Based on outside appearances, prosperity and happiness followed Rueben and Lillian no matter what venture they attempted. Although in love with Rose, Rueben was fond of Lillian; she was now nearly nineteen years old and her already extensive life experiences had given her an air of boldness and confidence not often seen in young women her age. Although she had her faults, Rueben thought she had an aptitude for business that would be beneficial to him.

Just twenty years old, Rueben, too, disclosed an air of success and confidence, a demeanor attributed, by those who knew him well, to a childhood in a home of art, education, politics, and business.

As a couple, Rueben and Lillian made a striking duo. Heads turned wherever they went, and socially, both Rueben and Lillian were accomplished dancers. They spent many evenings practicing the newest steps, and Rueben purchased a Victrola as a gift for Lillian. The tall, wooden cabinet housing of the music machine, placed in Lillian's front parlor, stood as evidence of his increasing prosperity.

Several of the latest dance steps required Lillian to become physically close to Rueben, and one evening, while practicing a new dance move, Rueben realized Lillian was struggling to control her passions. The dance was a Brazilian tango, and its moves brought her body close to his. The hypnotic music and sensual moves may have caused passion to arise within her, and he heard her whisper, "Rueben," in his ear as he dipped her. In such a close embrace, she passionately kissed him, and Rueben brought her to a standing position and softly pushed her away.

"Lillian," he said. "Now is not the time." He led her to a small divan. "Remember," he said. "We talked about this. We want to wait until we're married before we..."

"I know what I told you," she said. "If only my body would agree with me."

"Just take your time, my dear. We have plenty of time."

Rueben looked into Lillian's teary eyes, and in his mind, he embraced Rose. Fantasy was the only way he could carry out his pretense of passion toward Lillian. He'd tried, really tried, to convince himself that he could love Lillian, and seeing that she was in tears and her shaking body, Rueben held her close to calm her, but his mind drifted to a dance held long ago in Rivers Edge, the little town near Rose's farmstead. He remembered it was a wedding dance, and all the neighbors within the township were there. Rose, about thirteen, had just begun to show her female shape, and when he asked for a waltz, she first said no, but her friends urged her on. As they waltzed, he swore he would make her his wife, no matter what. That was the night he fell in love. He was saving himself for Rose.

Rueben suddenly recoiled at the thought of an accidental sexual mishap with Lillian. He didn't need any kind of scandal that may be destructive to his business and political plans. "I really must go now, Lillian," he said. "I will see you at the mercantile tomorrow. Have a good night." Rueben gave her a quick kiss on the forehead and left.

The relationship would be nothing more than friendship. Still, she was fun company, and it was going to be a long winter in St. Giles as the only single man, save for a few railroad men who traveled through on occasion.

Rueben decided his next great venture in St. Giles would be to build a new dance hall. With the little town growing, and with the river about to freeze over for the winter, Rueben decided to get the ballroom up as quickly as possible. At the time, he didn't know that building the dance hall would become the biggest mistake of his entire life.

Anna
October 1911

Her Lakota name was Ptaysanwee, meaning White Buffalo. She was born on the Standing Rock Indian Reservation. As a child, at an early age, she was sent to the church boarding school for girls. It was there that she learned sewing, reading, and writing. It was also where she felt the first sting of a strap and the backside of a paddle.

Anna Crow Wing was forced to stay in school most of the year. On occasion, she was allowed home for a rare visit. She spent time with her grandmother, a well-known medicine woman and a seer of visions, and it was a time of hope. Anna's grandmother told her that she saw many gifts in Anna, and she taught Anna much about the earth, and spent many hours teaching medicines. When she was only twelve years old, Anna helped her grandmother to deliver a baby. When Anna ran away from the church boarding school, her grandmother hid her from the schoolmaster. Secretly, Anna remained true to her native religion and did not want to have anything to do with the church religion that threatened her with beatings if she did not obey its commands. To raise money for the school during lean times, Anna was "lent out" to white families in the summer as domestic labor.

Anna's father had been a strong brave. He was killed in one of the many battles with the white man. Afterward, her mother died trying to keep her family alive. The last time Anna saw her, she was carrying a large load of wood on her back for heating the crude one-room log shack where the family of six had lived. Her people had tried to tell reservation officers that buffalo-hide tipis were more resistant to cold weather than leaky log shanties, which they were forced to build. One winter night, a raging blizzard caused the shanty chimney to back draft. This caused the fire to go out. Short of wood to restart the fire, Anna's mother went out in search of more logs to keep the fire going, but she never returned. Anna covered her younger brothers and sisters with her body to keep them warm in the freezing room. The following day, a neighbor opened the door to tell her that her mother had been found. She had fallen face down and froze to death. Others came to get the smaller children, and all of them were taken to be raised by different families. Anna wanted to keep the family together, but she was only fifteen years old.

The white man who came to the reservation in search of a wife offered to marry Anna. He was the first person to begin calling her by the name Anna. He could not pronounce her Indian name, so he shortened it. He promised to bring her and her brothers and sisters to his farm off the reservation, where they could live together. The promise he made to her is the reason why she agreed to marry him.

Anna believed the man. It was not that she wanted to marry a white man, but she did so out of necessity to help her family. He did follow through with his promise and brought the family to a run-down farmstead near St. Giles, but within six months, he left them, never to be heard from again. Although destitute, Anna knew how to live from Mother Earth, and within a short time, she had a vegetable garden and hunted deer, and she processed them for winter. Despite being shunned from most social activities within the community, Anna became someone that area inhabitants came to rely on. They called on her for midwifery and for her abilities to produce garden vegetables and healthy livestock. She was sought out for her natural medicines and for weather predictions. Rumors about her strange spiritual practices instilled fear and respect into her neighbors.

Now, Anna found her way to the tall hilltop behind her home, her sacred place. She pulled her shawl around her shoulders and shivered as she felt the change of seasons in her bones. She carefully watched for cacti because she didn't want to catch the fringe of her prayer shawl on their needles. She looked down from the high bluff, where at one time, the braves chased the buffalo to their death at the bottom of the cliff. There, the women awaited the dying beasts with knives and with pottery to process their meat for winter.

Anna placed her flattened hand across her eyes to shield them from the rising sun. It made a glorious appearance from the east, and from this direction, she sought the morning star for wisdom. The winding blue ribbon of the river reached the twin peak buttes beyond, and the buttes appeared to change from pink to lavender in the early morning light. The trees along the river had turned to fall colors, reds and golds.

She reached for her medicine bag. The small items inside represented the four elements of the earth: ashes for fire, dried plants for water, feathers for air, and rocks, which were actually arrowheads from her father, for earth.

She stretched out her arms toward the rising sun, and fell into a trance. She imagined her drab cotton dress to be soft deer skin, and her black hair fell loose and blew about her face. She felt the rush of the wind, and the spirit of Tatanka, the great buffalo, pass by.

After finishing her prayer, Anna paused on a large boulder to do her wisdom thinking. Her younger brothers and sisters had left the farm to move to South Dakota. With no one to care for, Anna had befriended Lillian after Lillian was sent away from her family for being pregnant.

She is a strange wasicu, Anna thought. She struggled to understand the young white woman and felt pity for her. Anna saw that Lillian needed protection, not just from the people around her, but also from herself.

The New Dance Hall
October 1911

O n a cool autumn morning, Rueben circled his newly completed dance hall. He stood in the gusty wind and admired
the long, wood structure. He'd built the hall in the center
of St. Giles and strategically next to the two-story frame house that
served as a boarding house and small restaurant. The boarding
house and restaurant is where he had first met Lillian and admired
her physical appearance and her work skills even more so. During
conversations, he'd soon discovered the close friendship Lillian had
with Rose, and she told him how Rose and her family grew in friendship over the years. He wondered how he'd never met Lillian prior to
then, and she pointed out that most of the time their families socialized during church functions. Ah, yes, then he understood.

Rueben had offered to purchase the boarding house from its
owner, who was an aging widow. He imagined what a profitable
combination his dance hall and that business would present in the
near future. Today would be an exciting day, he knew, because there
would be a cornerstone-laying celebration. Although mostly made
of wood, the foundation for the building would be brick, and today, Rueben's fellow Masons would be present for the ceremony. He
didn't expect many people from the community to attend because of
the Catholic ban against membership in the Masons.

Alcohol, though now illegal, was bound to become legalized in
the near future, Rueben knew. His father talked about it at length

during dinner parties with his friends, and with the railroad and the increase of farming in the area, Rueben's investors urged him to prepare for the time when the little community of St. Giles would be a bustling city. These advisors were also eager to come to St. Giles socially, away from public scrutiny, because most were well-known politicians. Rueben believed he understood what that meant, but he was determined not to let his establishment become like those he'd heard about in South Dakota. He liked having the support of his father's investors, but at times he disliked talking about his business with them. It seemed their subtle, secondary conversations implied he should do some things that weren't quite legal, and he recalled the evening he was initiated into the Masonic Temple in Bismarck. Men he always believed were enemies participated together in the ceremonies, as though they were long-lost brothers.

Always interested in a profitable business, Rueben didn't miss how Lillian's baking and herbal medicine business was becoming more and more lucrative. He'd urged her to work at the boarding house only part-time so that she could concentrate on her confectionaries. He offered to help financially so she could do so, and his plan was to hire Lillian full-time at the boarding house as the manager when he did purchase it. Already, when there was a special occasion—such as the upcoming Halloween Gala—Lillian had promised to assist with the cooking for the widow-owner until a replacement for her could be found.

Rueben, too, asked Lillian to manage the refreshment kitchen at the new dance hall for any upcoming social occasions, including today's cornerstone ceremony. Afterward, there would be socializing, and he told Lillian he understood her religious beliefs about the Masons, and that she would not be required to participate in any way. Besides, the ceremony was strictly men-only. In return, Lillian and Anna would be allowed to use the modernized kitchen in the dance hall for their own purposes, and the arrangement would work out well, because Lillian's kitchen in her small house didn't allow ample room for Anna and Lillian to preserve and prepare their remedies.

After the cornerstone ceremony on the morning of Halloween, Rueben invited Lillian for a final inspection of the dance hall before the Grand Opening Halloween Dance. "Lillian, here it is finally finished!" he said. "I must thank you for your wonderful food preparation for the ceremony."

Lillian untied her apron and placed it over her arm. She looked toward the church and uttered a prayer of protection in her mind, as she had done all day long while preparing the Masons' lunch. "Rueben, I so respect and admire you," she said. "But what a strange group that is with their uniforms and white aprons. What does it all mean?"

"Lillian, is it any stranger than what you see up there on the hill during any Mass?" he asked. "Doesn't Fr. Logan wear colorful robes? And when the bishop visits, I hear people kiss his ring. Don't you think that's a bit odd?"

Lillian nodded in agreement. She wondered if her father had heard about all this.

The Halloween Dance
October 1911

With the cornerstone laid, the dance hall was completed in time for the large, public Halloween Ball, which promised to be a huge success. Earlier in the week, Lillian and Anna had chatted while preparing food for the dance.

"Brrr, it's cold in here this morning," Lillian said as she put more firewood into the cast-iron cook stove. "Anna, do you think we'll have bad weather for the dance?"

"I saw the caterpillar this summer," Anna said while kneading bread dough. "It had narrow rings and they weren't black. That means we'll have a mild winter. There are also fewer bullberries on the trees, so that also means a warmer winter. But there can be a storm anytime." In North Dakota, Halloween weather can be whatever Mother Earth wants it to be. With her knowledge of plants and animals, Anna was the local weather forecaster.

When Halloween arrived, as predicted, the weather was cool, but clear. Guests arrived from all the little towns up and down the west side of the river. Because the possibility of an early, mid-autumn freeze might form and release ice chunks to float in the fast current, crossing the Missouri River from the east side on rafts or canoes carried risks. The narrow point at Gwyther, seven miles south of St. Giles, was the safest location to cross, and from that point, dance-goers could find friends willing to drive them to St. Giles. With no laws or restrictions, dances tended to last into the wee hours of the morning, as long as the musicians were willing to play. Many dance-goers planned ahead to stay overnight and to fulfill their All Saint's Day holy day obligation at the small wood-framed church in St. Giles. Because of the unusually mild weather, those who could not find indoor accommodations planned to camp out under wagons or in neighboring barns. The boarding house had been booked long in advance.

Because of Halloween, Lillian knew that the candy she made would be in high demand, not only for the dance, but also for Bismarck and Mandan Halloween social activities. She wrote Rose in September to ask if she could stay a few days and help with confection-making, and Rose replied that she would be delighted because she'd decided not to pursue a teaching position in Bismarck until after Christmas. She explained that her mother had taken a turn for the worse and was extremely weakened by all her female problems. Her father was struggling with her mother's female problems; he was having a difficult time understanding all the extremes in her behavior, and he really needed a woman around the house to help with cooking, canning, and preparing for winter. Rose said Papa felt bad she wasn't able to go to Bismarck to teach in the fall, but he was willing to let her visit Lillian for a few days if Ben made sure she got there and back again safely.

Ben was thrilled about having to escort Rose to St. Giles to help with confectionary baking. He saw it as an opportunity to build up his inventory before the big dance. The unusually mild autumn played to Ben's advantage because he'd been worried about the river freezing. He'd been trying to connive a way to make trips to St. Giles, and he and Anton had planned to use the excuse they were making trips to blacksmith shops and the mercantile there. However, other than a few mild frosts, the river hadn't started to freeze over yet, and the timely invitation Rose had received from Lillian allowed Anton, Ben, and his Indian help to make several legitimate trips across the river on Old Joe's raft.

Ben, Anton, and Big Red had spent many nights down at the still, and Big Red—the nickname given to the Indian ranch hand whom Chris had employed nearly year-round—now worked as a distiller for Ben.

Ben had made a couple spurious batches early in his "cooking" days. The faultily distilled batches had made his "rotgut" dangerously impure and had caused one customer to almost die; he was still paralyzed. Lawbreakers don't usually bring in the law in such situations, but Ben constantly looked over his shoulder to be sure the fellow's family wasn't out to get even with him. Fortunately, this latest batch went very well.

After all had been bottled and quality-tested during sampling, they individually wrapped the corked, flat-glass flasks in burlap and tucked them into the tops of their boots for transport. Big Red had talked his brothers into helping with the bootlegging in exchange for a few bottles of their own, and Ben approved, because they weren't interested in making money—they only wanted product—but they were mostly drunk when they helped. Ben, knowing how whiskey quickly took over a man's soul, rarely drank it himself.

Ben told Rose that he and Anton planned to camp out during the night of the Halloween dance. He knew that Halloween night would be extremely busy and lucrative and sleep would be the least of his concerns. He would focus his energy on turning a pretty penny using spirits of his own.

Knowing Rueben still had intentions of courting Rose ate at Ben, and the nearness of Rueben to Rose during days prior to the dance concerned him. When this party is over, he thought, I'm going to have to concentrate on bringing him down. Ben knew plenty of good information about Rueben's old man and his high-powered friends. And he'd have to take care of Anton, too. If only he didn't have to pay him off. Anton was a wood tick on Ben's neck, continuously sucking him dry.

On a positive note, Rose was beginning to come around. Ben chuckled at how Rose meekly asked for his permission after she received the invite from Lillian. He was quite sure that even though the delivery method was crude, Rose had gotten the message: She was to be in agreement with his wishes as her beau. Following the argument on the riverbank, she seemed to have changed, and lately, she seemed more compliant. He found that his tougher stance with her had given better results, and when she disagreed about anything, he noticed that a hard squeeze to her arm or even a quick pinch to her cheek caused tears, but it improved her behavior. He just had to make sure that he reprimanded her out of sight of her family. There was no more talk of school-teaching, to his relief.

The night before Ben was to take Rose to St. Giles, he personally gathered up a large quantity of bottled brew, packed as much as he could get into his saddle bags, and led his horse down to the riverbank. There, he hid the cargo deep into the undergrowth of bushes and trees and heaps of fallen leaves. He planned to deliver the load himself the next day. He was beginning to dislike how much liquor his help was consuming.

Under a nearly full moon, Ben rode his horse back to the barn. He crept quietly into the house and went to his attic room. He lay back and looked into the rafters of the pointed roof and thought about the day he and Rose would sleep in the large bed in the master bedroom below.

Ben chuckled when he thought about the night Anton unwillingly helped him carry his belongings into the attic. The night of the move, Anton made some kind of comment about his father killing the fatted calf, whatever that meant. Sometimes Ben felt a twinge of guilt about Chris. He had to admit the old man was good to him, but he saw other men as either customers or enemies. Chris didn't seem to fit either category, so he labeled him as someone to be used.

Ben was fairly certain Mary was losing her mind. She'd run outside in the middle of the night to "cool off" and her uncontrollable outbursts toward anyone who was not following her demands was grating. Her constant crying was enough to make him want to take his kerchief and wrap it around her mouth. The only time she seemed normal was when her baby boy, Anton, was close by. The two of them were sickening, the way she coddled him.

The following morning, Rose, Anton, and Ben made their way to the riverbank for the trip to St. Giles. It was cool and steam rose from the water. The Indian name for the river, Smokey Waters, seemed fitting.

After crossing the river, Anton and Ben left Rose in Lillian's care. They checked on the spot they'd staked out for their speakeasy and the alcohol stashed there; no one would suspect the horse barn behind the one-room schoolhouse, which was just uphill from the dance hall. It was close enough to keep customers happy, and far enough away to avoid suspicion. In addition, men's and women's outhouses were close by and would allow for an excuse to leave the dance. Ben's customers were mostly men, but a few women liked to sip now and then, and the gals told him strong drink made personal relations with men more tolerable.

Ben liked the Halloween holiday because no one could easily

guess who was who in costume, unless they were very well-known. This allowed for those who might not normally indulge in a drink to do so. He'd even known prohibitionists to chance a snort at a costume ball. If he could get them feeling the fire of his brew in their blood, he might add them to his customer list.

Ben and Anton didn't put a lot of thought into their costumes; they didn't have time for that. Already wearing large-brimmed, western style hats and leather vests, Ben suggested they simply pull red-patterned handkerchiefs over their faces and cast themselves as robbers. No one would question the gun belts and six shooters at their sides.

Rose had found clothes from her grandmother stored in the attic and decided to dress up as a pioneer woman. Changing into her costume for Lillian to see, she put on a high-collared, white-cotton blouse with a cameo pin at the neck. She added a long, black wool skirt, and arranged her hair in a bun. She tied a printed bonnet over her hair and covered her eyes with a pair of wire-rimmed spectacles.

"Lillian, what am I?"

"Rose, you're a school teacher, as always," Lillian guessed, unimpressed. In her bedroom, she opened a large brown box filled with taffeta dresses. "Guess what I plan to be," she said.

"A princess."

"No. A few adjustments will give you a better idea."

When Lillian tore the sleeves out of a lovely red taffeta gown, Rose was mortified. "What are you doing? You are destroying a perfectly good gown!"

Lillian explained she was given the box of old dresses by the owner of the boarding house. The aging widow was once an opera singer, but she had no more use for the dresses. She slipped into the now-sleeveless gown and folded down the neckline to expose a generous amount of cleavage. She reached into her dresser drawer and placed a corset over the top of the bodice, and finally, she cut the front of skirt to reveal her legs from the knees down. Rose ran from window to window to be sure the curtains were pulled tightly closed.

"I'm not nearly finished," Lillian said. "Follow me to the powder room."

Mesmerized, Rose followed obediently, but she wasn't prepared for Lillian's final addition to the costume: Lillian applied bright red rouge and lip color unabashedly to her cheeks and face.

"Lillian!" Rose scolded. "You certainly aren't going out in public dressed like that! Rueben will be very embarrassed."

Rueben dressed in the outfit Lillian had compiled for him earlier in the week. She told him his costume would complement hers. He took care to put the outfit on just as she told him. She'd decided he should wear a suit with a brightly colored neckerchief and a vest of red brocade silk, which would match her dress. He viewed himself in his shaving mirror and decided he looked like a real dandy. He took the charcoal pencil Lillian had provided and drew a single-line mustache, curled at the ends.

Rueben walked across the yard toward Lillian's home to escort both Lillian and Rose to the dance. He wondered what the ladies would be wearing, and stepped back, stunned, when Lillian emerged from the door. Speechless about how to address Lillian, he complemented Rose first. "Rose, no matter what or how you dress, you are stunningly beautiful." As he finished his last word, Lillian brushed past him and hurried to the dance hall.

"Excuse me, Rose," he said. "Can you see yourself to the dance hall? I better catch up with Lillian for the Grand Opening procession. We are to lead out."

Rueben caught up to a perturbed Lillian. "I'm so sorry," he said. "Your beautiful sight left me without words. You're the belle of this ball. Listen, the music is starting."

The dance started at eight o'clock sharp. Rueben and Lillian led the procession, followed by anyone else in costume that cared to participate. Comments were made about how Rueben and Lillian made a striking couple. Many thought they looked as though they'd stepped out of the Moulin Rouge.

Without a partner for the procession, Rose wandered to the kitchen. One or two of Lillian's chocolates made her feel better in short time.

The music started out lively, and although most of the dancers enjoyed traditional polkas and waltzes because of their largely German heritage, a new kind of music was being introduced. Rose watched as Rueben and Lillian, who had been practicing some new dances, taught others how they were done. The music was called Ragtime, and the band knew how to play only a limited amount of the new numbers, and promised to learn more of the new music for future dances.

As the music played on, Rose wondered about the amount of time Ben was spending out of the dance hall. He had appeared and danced a few rounds with her, but then disappeared for the longest time. Anton would also appear and dance a few rounds with her, and then he, too, would disappear. However, between Ben and Anton, she always seemed to have a dance partner.

As the evening grew closer to midnight, some of the dancers became increasingly lively and loud, while others slept on the long benches that lined the dance floor. It appeared as though the party would last until the wee hours of the morning. Rueben and Lillian were totally unaware of the news that had spread about "refreshments" in the barn behind the school.

And then, the local sheriff and his deputy strode into the dance hall. The deputy had a poster in his hand, and he and the sheriff stepped onto the stage and demanded the band stop playing. The sheriff announced that they were looking for a man with light hair and piercing blue eyes, and after examining the poster, Lillian motioned Rueben to follow her to the kitchen. "Does that drawing resemble Ben Hofts?" she asked.

Rueben shrugged his shoulders. He walked back to the sheriff. "What is this man wanted for?" he asked.

The sheriff answered loudly for all to hear. "He's been running corn whiskey at gatherings such as this," he said. "He ran a couple of bad batches, too, and almost killed some folk. I want him put away. Furthermore, if anyone is caught drinking anything illegal, that person will be arrested, as well."

Anton moved toward the dance hall for his turn to dance with Rose. Ben wanted to make sure she had no opportunities to dance with Rueben, so he made Anton dance with her when he was busy with customers. Between the two, Rose danced with no one else.

When Anton noticed the lawmen enter the dance hall, he ran back to the barn to warn Ben. They wrapped all the empty flasks into the burlap rags, hustled everyone out of the barn, pulled their handkerchiefs over their faces like bandits, and went into the dance hall. They walked right past the sheriff and his deputy.

Ben found Rose and led her out a side door. "Rose, I really want to turn in so I can get to Mass early tomorrow," he said. He offered his arm and led her quickly to Lillian's house, where he gave her a kiss before letting her inside. With Rose safe, Ben ran as fast as he could to recover the flasks he'd hid under the hay in the barn.

The sheriff and the deputy walked around the dance hall with a lantern. They began looking into parked vehicles and into wagons. Ben held his breath when he saw the lantern start to move toward the barn. Flasks wrapped in rags in burlap sacks still made noise. He wondered where Anton had gone, and the Indian help were nowhere to be found. He moved slowly around the backside of the barn and crept his way down to the men's outhouse. The sheriff and deputy reached the barn and looked in the stalls and in the hayloft. Finding nothing, the duo headed toward the men's outhouse. Inside and with the door locked, there was only one thing Ben could do. He dropped the bottles into the toilet hole and then he pretended to make use of the facility. He finished his "job" and then stepped out to face the lawmen. "Evening, Sheriff," he said.

The sheriff nodded, and went inside to use the toilet. Ben shuddered at the thought of pulling that bag out of the hole again.

Finally, the lawmen got into their vehicle and drove north toward Mandan. Disgusted, Ben went into the toilet and pulled up the sack. He threw it into the water trough near the barn. He looked for Anton. When he finally found him at the blacksmith shop, he discovered Anton had gotten himself into a quandary. He'd set up a dice game, with himself as the main player, and had lost his money in the short amount of time Ben had been covering their tracks. And instead of hiding the inventory, he'd drunk a good portion of the moonshine with the smithy. Ben grabbed Anton by the collar, and he threw him against the wall of the building. The two struggled until

Anton promised to pay back what he'd drunk.

Under the cover of darkness, the bootleggers gathered their flasks and hid them down by the river. Ben told Anton that the holidays in Bismarck, from Thanksgiving through New Year's Eve, was his most profitable time, and that the still would have to run full-time through then. Ben needed someone to cover deliveries, and he told Anton he could be part of the business, but he'd better not pull another stunt like he did that night, or he'd kill him. The two wandered back toward the now quiet town, and opened their bedrolls. They slept under a wagon, Ben with one hand on his gun, and the other on his vest pocket. Because he'd had enough to drink, Anton slept soundly until he felt Ben kick him to wake up.

The following morning, while the tired faithful attended early morning All Saint's Day Mass, Ben struggled to stay alert to impress Rose. He thought it was nothing short of torture to listen to a rosary followed by a long line of confessions. Many of those confessing had enjoyed some real tongue-loosening the night before, and Ben figured if they told the priest what they'd shared with him, there'd be some long penances. Ben entertained himself by winking at the offenders as they strode back to their pews following confession. Anton fell asleep in the back pew.

Rueben didn't attend Mass with Lillian. He had to open the mercantile early to catch customers on their way home. It wasn't really worth the effort, however, because Catholics wouldn't shop on a holy day, anyway. The inactivity gave him time to let his mind wander. He imagined dancing with Rose. She'd looked so pure and innocent in her pioneer costume.

Rueben was deep in thought when he heard the store door creak open. Anna stood in the doorway, her shape outlined by the sun that poured in around her. She stared angrily at Rueben, and her stern voice matched her facial features as she spoke. "Rueben, you are not an honest man," she said. "You are not being honest with Lillian. I see great lack of truth in your heart. I will not allow you to hurt my friend. Tell Lillian the truth about your feelings. If you don't, I will do what is right."

The Betrothal
October 1911

The first snowstorm of the season came before Thanksgiving, and the storm created problems for the Welsley farm. The snow made it difficult to get from the house to the barn to check on the horses and to supply the cattle with hay. Earlier in the fall, they'd been moved into a tree-protected gully for wintering. Now, the hired men attempted to keep the area clear for spring calving by pushing manure into large piles to create a wind-protected area.

The early storm had trapped the Welsley family and Ben in the house most evenings for a week. It was too dangerous to venture out in the dark, and during the daytime was sometimes difficult, as well. Chris and Ben spent time studying the Catechism and preparing for Ben's baptism, which was planned for after Advent in January. Rose and Mary passed the time by working on crocheted doilies, tablecloths, and other handmade crafts to share as Christmas gifts, and the needlework seemed to have a calming effect on Mary. Ben and Anton, too distrustful to allow the other out of his sight, became fidgety, and decided to make a batch of moonshine and, as soon as the weather would allow, to run it to Bismarck for holiday parties. Spending much of their time squabbling, they grew impatient waiting for the weather to clear up so they could reach the still.

Ben roused Anton from his sleep in the middle of the night. "Anton, get up, you lazy good-for-nuthin," he said. "You still owe me, so let's get down to the shack and get cooking."

Anton rolled over. "You get down there and get things going, and I'll be down shortly."

Ben yanked back the covers and pulled Anton to a standing position. He faced him nose to nose, and sputtered, "Get your clothes on, now! Or you'll fall back asleep for the last time."

As soon as he felt the prick from the knife Ben had opened and held to his belly, Anton quickly grabbed his clothes.

As Anton dressed, Ben sat on the end of the bed and looked around the room. That's when he noticed the framed oval portrait of a younger Mary Welsley sitting on the floor. Looking up the wall, where it may have fallen from, he noticed a small crack below the nail used for hanging the portrait. It was on the wall that separated Rose's room from Anton's.

"Why, you no-good, rotten…" Ben grabbed Anton by his hair and pulled him up. "You animal," he said. "Just one more thing to hold over your head, you lousy excuse for a man. Let's get this done before I do something you'll regret."

The two quietly crept out of the house and down to the barn. They gathered their supplies, and the moon reflected brightly off the snow and lit their way down to the still. When they were out of earshot of the house, Anton retaliated. "You have no cause to call the pot black," he said. "You think I don't know about you sneaking off to Bismarck? You ain't got no right snarling at me for taking a peek once in a while. At least I ain't touchin'. I know you don't give a hoot about Rose one way or another except for gettin' in good with the old man, so whaddya care? Are you getting sweet on her? Well, she ain't gonna get the farm, no matter what."

They spent the night cooking mash. After a few days, the corn, sugar, and yeast concoction would be ready to heat up and run through the distiller. Ben knew the secret to good corn whiskey was all about timing. He wondered, *Maybe I should just let Anton sam-*

ple the first whiskey that comes out of the still. He probably wouldn't know that those first few ounces are enough to send him straight to Hell, or if he's lucky, to blind him so that he can't enjoy his favorite peephole pastime. No, I need to keep him around a little longer. I'll plan a notable farewell when the time comes. Sooner or later, he'll more than likely get into a gambling deal that'll end up being his last game.

Ben's distrust had grown so deep that he no longer let Anton see where the final jugs of fine whiskey were hid. His next hurdle was to find a way to get the holiday shipment north to Bismarck.

The next morning at breakfast, Ben asked, "Mr. Welsley, after the weather clears up, could I escort Rose to Bismarck for a day of shopping and to an opera house play?"

"Quit calling me Mr. Welsley. 'Chris' is good enough. It'll be fine as long as the weather holds and Anton rides along. The weather can change quickly, and if you get stuck, you might need an extra man to help with the horses. There's so much snow that I prefer you to take a team and the sleigh."

Rose asked, "Can I send a note to Lillian to see if she and Rueben would like to join us?"

Ben recoiled, but then had a better idea: He could use some time to make deliveries and the couple would be a distraction for Rose. "Certainly," he said. "After the play, we could meet them for dinner, but it will be a very late evening for a ride back to the farm in the dark."

"I have friends from St. Mary's who would be happy to extend an overnight room to Anton and Rose," Chris said. "Ben, I'm sure they could find a spare room for you, as well."

"No need to worry about me," Ben said. "I have old friends from the railroad who have been pestering me to come up for a visit." He stood up from the table. "Then it's all set," he said. "We just need to find a good time for everyone."

That evening, after everyone had gone to bed, Ben went to Chris to ask him for Rose's hand in marriage. To make the best possible impression, he'd been practicing his betrothal speech.

"Mr. Welsley," he started. "Sorry, Chris," he said. "As you know, I'm very fond of your daughter. I come here tonight to ask for her hand in marriage. I promise to be a loving and good husband."

Chris looked surprised, but then pleased. "Ben," he said, "I must have you promise one thing before I say, 'Yes.' You have to promise you'll be baptized and confirmed as a Catholic. Easter is when most converts are baptized, after the new holy water is blessed. If you agree to this, then I'll agree to your request."

Ben agreed emphatically, and the betrothal agreement was worked out. He couldn't have been more pleased. The conditions were laid out verbally: Chris said he'd leave all the property to Rose as her dowry, and Ben and Rose would take care of Mary if she outlived her husband. Anton could stay on the farm as a partner, and he would receive one-third of the income generated. If Anton left the farm for any reason, he couldn't expect to be taken back as a partner. The two men shook hands heartily.

Two weeks later, with whiskey wrapped in burlap sacks and loaded into the two-seat sleigh, Ben, Anton, and Rose set out for Bismarck, bundled up warmly for the ride, and sitting together in the front seat for warmth. Oddly, the blizzard that had caused so many problems on the east side of the river left very little snow on the west side, just as Anna had predicted by the caterpillar.

Lillian and Rueben agreed to meet up with the trio in Bismarck.

They were able to take his auto over the frozen dirt road, and when they reached Bismarck, the Missouri River was adequately frozen, so they were able to cross easily on the ice. The drive across was unnerving, and as the tires slipped, the cracking ice frightened Lillian. She hung on to Rueben's arm in fear and held her breath until they reached the other side. Once there, the automobile could scarcely make the incline toward the city center.

Coming from the east side, Ben, Anton, and Rose didn't face crossing a river, but they did have hard-packed snow banks to cross. The sure-footed draft horses easily pulled the sleigh over the hardened snow, which caused the bottles to clink on occasion. "Ben, what was that sound?" Rose asked as she looked around the sleigh for the source.

"That was just icicles breaking from the bottom of the sleigh," Ben said. He pulled the team to a stop. "Anton, go underneath and break them off so that they don't bother Rose," he said. Anton jumped from the burgundy button seat and reached below. He pretended to knock off the icicles and then hopped back onto the sleigh and adjusted a tarp in the back seat while Rose paid no attention.

Ben pulled the team and sleigh to a livery on the south side of the railroad station. Anton unhooked the team while Ben dropped coins into the hands of a young man who looked as though he were sixteen. He took him aside and pretended to give him some final instructions, and the young man smiled broadly at Ben and began to brush down the horses.

The group met at the Hotel McKenzie to make their plans. As they stood outside in the cold on Main Street, Rose and Lillian linked arms to window-shop. While they were enjoying the latest winter fashions in a store window, a woman brushed past them and strolled up to the men. The girls watched the woman with annoy-ance, because she talked and laughed and appeared to know all three of the men. "Who is that?" Rose asked.

"You don't want to know," Lillian replied. "Let's go rescue the men." She walked briskly back to Rueben's side, took his arm in hers, and led him down the street.

Rose stared at Ben, and she noticed he appeared very uncom-fortable. Anton appeared to be enjoying the situation. When the woman spoke, her words seemed to curl in the cold air. "Well, Ben, dear, who is this?" she asked, examining Rose. "Why, she looks like she just stepped out of a schoolmarm picture catalog!"

Ben, shifting his weight from one side to the other, replied, "Sally, this is my fiancée, Miss Rose Welsley." Rose bristled, stunned. Since when did I become his fiancée? she wondered, but ever the polished lady, she answered calmly, trying to be cordial, "My pleasure," she said and glared at Ben.

"Oh, no! Bumping into Ben and his… fiancée… is always my pleasure," Sally purred back and reached out her black-laced glove to touch Ben's elbow. She held it with a little too much familiarity, and then walked away with an exaggerated amount of sway to her stride. The strong scent of her perfume seemed to trail after her.

When she was out of earshot, Rose turned to Ben. "I am not your fiancée," she said. "I really would like to hear more about your strange friend. Why, you look quite uncomfortable!" She turned to ask Anton if he'd met Sally before, but Anton was nowhere to be seen. Ben suggested Lillian and Rose continue their shopping and offered each lady a few paper bills to enjoy themselves.

As Ben and Rueben watched the girls walk off, the two men agreed to act civilly toward each other for the duration of the visit.

Ben urgently needed to figure out a way to lose Rueben for an hour or more to make his deliveries, and it seemed Anton had found a way to occupy his time for a while. Seeing the red-and-white barber pole in front of one of his regular customer's establishments, Ben devised a plan to distract Rueben. "Rueben," he said, "I say we get our ugly mugs cleaned up for the ladies this evening."

"Speak for yourself," Rueben said.

"Sir, we planned to be civil this evening," Ben said. "The shave and haircut are on me. You go first."

The barber motioned Rueben to sit down, and Ben slipped the barber extra coins to dawdle the time for Rueben's shave. Rueben relaxed, and soon he dozed off in the barber's chair.

Ben now had his chance to get his flasks and to arrange transport to his waiting customers. This was the most difficult and dangerous part of his business, but it was the thrill and adrenaline rush that Ben craved. First, he had to attend to his "granny fees," the pay-offs to the local police willing to accept them. Then, he had to dodge the revenuers. In some ways, winter made things easier, with large coats to hide bulky bottles, but sneaking off into alleys and to obvious places a runner would go was not Ben's style. Besides, there was another danger involved in those places: other bootleggers, those who'd rather not distill their own, and who lurked in alleys and dark corners to rob unsuspecting runners.

Ben used a variety of clever ways to distribute his product. One such way was to employ a variety of bottles that previously held hair tonics, castor oil, or even milk. He painted the outsides of the bottles the color of what was *supposed* to be on the inside so that the brew could be peddled through the front doors by street-smart runners disguised as legitimate salesmen. Ben tried not to deliver the product himself, and his runners wouldn't dare cross him, because all he'd had to do was make an example out of one, and no one dared try it again. Too bad, he thought. That kid was only twelve years old when they found him lying on the railroad tracks.

When he heard the ruckus, Rueben woke abruptly in the barber's chair. All the barbershop patrons ran to the window to see what was going on. Down the block, a fist fight was in progress, and it appeared as though a group of juvenile-aged boys were in a street fight. Soon, the local police surrounded the rowdy young men, but it took the lawmen quite some time to settle them down. Rueben swore under his breath and returned back to the barber's chair and to his daydreams of Rose.

Ben glanced down the street to watch the progress of the disruption. Organizing a faux fight to divert the law was a bit costly, but so much more could be accomplished by having the police occupied. While the police tried to subdue the brawl, he watched his hired runners move about the street to distribute alcohol.

With a pocket full of money, Ben walked past the watch shop. He decided to purchase a ring for Rose as a betrothal gift. He chose a gold band with a beautiful, green emerald topped with a small crown of diamonds. He planned to give it to her at dinner to send a message to both Rueben and Anton that he had every intention of marrying Rose next spring.

Dinner was not pleasant. Lillian brought up the rude treatment she had received earlier in the year by Rueben's parents. The remarks she made angered him, so they stopped speaking to one another. Anton seemed restless and quite intoxicated. Rose seemed irritated about the scene with the woman on the street. The only person who had an air of gaiety about him was Ben.

When dinner was over, Ben stood and made his marriage proposal, which sounded more like an announcement. "Rose," he said. "I have asked permission from your father for your hand in marriage. He has agreed." He pulled a small, dark red velvet box from his pocket and opened the lid. He bent down on one knee, removed the ring from the box, and slid it on Rose's finger. He lifted her hand to his lips, and softly kissed it. "There, see, we are officially engaged!" he declared.

Rose said nothing. Lillian began to laugh. Anton looked as though he was going to lose his dinner and ran for the door. Rueben pounded the table with his fist, tears welling up. The other diners in the restaurant stood and clapped. Many rushed to the table to congratulate the newly engaged couple.

Christmas Dreams and Schemes
Winter 1911

Rueben made a decision: He would play the role of a man so powerfully attractive that Rose would come to her senses and break off her engagement with Ben. He would do everything in his power to convince her that she was making a terrible mistake.

The project of winning Rose would be a full-time, all-consuming act, and so Rueben considered how to use Lillian in the scheme. She was young and attractive, and she would eventually find someone else. He wasn't the type of man to string a woman along, but he considered it necessary to exploit Lillian by showing Rose the kind of husband he could be. The attentive, intelligent, wealthy Rueben hoped that Rose would realize what a mistake and mismatch her marriage to Ben would be. The principal challenge for Rueben would be patience and to endure the play-act of being a lover for Lillian.

In the end, Rueben was confident that Rose would break off her insane alliance with Ben, and even though Rueben would never be favorable in Chris Welsley's eyes, he didn't care about that. He only wanted Rose.

By December, the Missouri River had frozen solid. Families living on the east side of the river shopped Rueben's mercantile more frequently, and the Welsleys were often in St. Giles for supplies, church, or socializing. On occasion, Mary Welsley came to seek herbal remedies from Anna and Lillian, and Rose accompanied Mary during those trips.

During her visits, Rose noticed a remarkable change in Rueben. He unashamedly showed public affection toward Lillian, when previously, he seemed stand-offish and cool. He now paid special attention to Lillian's personal comfort, and made sure she had a cup of tea or was not too chilled. He listened intently to her every word, and never disagreed, no matter how ridiculous her opinions, and Rose was astounded by the content of their conversations: The couple discussed many interesting topics, including literature, music, art, and even politics. Rueben's involvement with Lillian deepened on subsequent visits, and sometimes Rose felt uncomfortable with their public displays of affection. Secretly, Rose felt covetous when Rueben would brush a soft kiss onto Lillian's cheek or near her ear. Ben had never seemed so tender. Envious, she watched as Rueben held Lillian's hand as they walked, and Rueben's compliments to Lillian never seemed to cease. He continually praised her about her fashion, cooking, or business knowledge, and Rose began to feel something ugly stirring deep inside. Was it jealousy? Lillian's independence had always made her jealous, but this felt different.

Rose thought about Ben; he couldn't carry an intelligent conversation if he tried. The only deep subject they had in common was the Catechism, but all he knew were the canned answers given for the questions for the upcoming test. Ben didn't know how to discuss deep feelings about God, and he certainly knew nothing about art and poetry. He never treated her tenderly unless he wanted something, like an extra goodnight kiss. He was sometimes rude to her, but as soon as they were in Papa's presence, he changed magically into a prince. Rose knew she was making a horrible mistake.

Lillian had been worried about Rueben's feelings, but after Rose's engagement to Ben, Rueben seemed like a different person. Whatever the cause for change, it didn't matter to Lillian. She was being treated like a queen. It seemed such a long time ago she'd lost her husband, Josef, and baby Adam. Her parents were finally talking to her again, and life was very good. At long last, she was beginning to feel at peace.

Anna said something strange to Lillian one day while they were baking chocolates and dainties for upcoming holiday parties. "Lillian, life is a large circle," she said. "In the circle of life, sometimes there are wolves. Watch out for them. Sometimes, they come in sheep's clothing."

"Anna, what are you talking about?"

"I'm not going to say any more. Sometimes, there is more wisdom in silence. I only hope that all this time we've spent together has taught you to be observant of life around you, including the man, Rueben."

Rueben felt sickened about his ongoing masquerade, but to his comfort, he noticed odd expressions on Rose's face whenever he played the part of attentive beau. When Rose was not around, he had to continue the façade due to the incessant number of letters Rose and Lillian exchanged back and forth. He wanted to be sure Lillian told Rose about his affection to her, and he schemed to implement his final knockout punch at Christmastime. If this strategy did not win her over, he would plan another way.

Socially, life was quiet in the little town of St. Giles during Advent. In Early December, Rueben had suggested they invite Rose and Ben for the Christmas celebration. In her latest letter, Rose said Ben wasn't happy about the invitation and wanted to spend their engaged holiday at the Welsley home, but long winter days had aggravated her mother's moods, and Rose felt overwhelmed with household chores. She didn't have the time or energy to plan and prepare a Christmas feast and looked forward to a day away from the farm. Rueben hurt for Rose.

When Christmas Day arrived cold, bright, and sunny, Rueben walked to the frozen river edge to wait for Ben and Rose. The view to the opposite side of the river was better in winter when the trees had no leaves. When they arrived in the sleigh, Ben begrudgingly shook Rueben's hand. Rose seemed afraid to look him in the eyes, and whispered, "Merry Christmas." Ben offered Rueben a ride back in the sleigh, and Rueben sat next to silent Rose. Rueben spoke first. "Lillian is excited about attending High Mass with you this morning," he said. "Look, there she is waving from the porch."

Rueben watched as Lillian and Rose embraced. He momentarily held a twinge of guilt for what he was doing to their friendship.

Rueben had gone to extravagant lengths to decorate and prepare a wonderful Christmas dinner party. He'd purchased Lillian an expensive red wool suit for the holiday, and during the time Rose, Ben, and Lillian attended High Mass, he set the table in beautiful china and laid a pair of silk gloves on Lillian's plate. He attached a little card that read, "If from glove, you take the letter 'g', then glove is love, and that I send to thee." Well, he thought, this should certainly break Rose's heart.

When the trio returned from Mass, they sat down at the beautifully arranged table. It seemed as though the celebration of the birth of the Christ Child had affected everyone's mood, even if they weren't true believers. Both Lillian and Rose stared at the gloves on the plate, and as Rueben surmised, Rose knew exactly what they signified from all of her literature readings. He'd planned this so well: They were a Victorian betrothal gift.

Lillian did not understand the glove's significance. She quickly slid them onto her hands and thought they were just another gift. "Oh Rueben, how exquisite," she said, "and they fit. What does this mean? It's strange you'd put them on my plate."

This time it was Rueben who got down on one knee. He proposed in a most poetic way to Lillian, and the emotion and beauty of the proposal caused Rose to break down in tears.

As soon as dinner ended, Rose asked Ben to take her home. She fumbled over excuses, such as having to take care of Mama, anything to get out of Lillian's house.

Lillian hugged Rose tightly as they said goodbye. "Rose, will you be the Matron of Honor at our wedding? I know we won't wait long. Rueben has told me he wants to marry on the most romantic day of the year, Valentine's Day. Oh, please say yes, so we can start planning."

"Lillian, I can't be your Matron of Honor if you don't get married in the Catholic Church. Besides, Valentine's Day is on Ash Wednesday next year, and you know that is the first day of Lent. Marriages aren't allowed during Lent. Papa would not allow it."

"I am sorry, I am cold standing here," she said. "Ben, please take me home."

In silence, Ben and Rose rode back to the Welsley farm. Rose's non-stop tears didn't go unnoticed.

"Rose, don't tell me you're in tears because you're happy about Lillian's engagement. Why, all Rueben came up with for her engagement gift was a cheap pair of gloves. Look at that ring on your finger and tell me, who's the better man?"

The slap Ben felt across his face came as a surprise. In defense, he returned a slap to Rose and with such force that it knocked her warm winter hat off her head. Ben pulled back hard on the reins to stop the horses, and he grabbed Rose. She fought against him and struggled to get out of the seat. Not strong enough, she broke down in sobs, and she allowed Ben to hold her and wipe away her tears.

After the fight with Ben in the sleigh, Rose decided she would play the part of the happily engaged woman, and she would play the part of the dutiful daughter. She would pretend to be a loving sister, and her most difficult act would be that of Lillian's best friend.

The Dance to End All Dances
1912

With Rueben engaged to Lillian, Ben felt relieved. He continued to collaborate with Anton to make moonshine and to supply customers during the holidays. After Advent, and between Christmas and Ash Wednesday, business would become hectic, and after the Hotel McKenzie will have celebrated its grand opening, alcohol and ladies of the evening would pass through tunnels beneath Bismarck on a regular basis.

After the holidays, Chris continued to trust Ben with his auto. The weather had been blizzard-like earlier in winter, but on New Year's Day and in the weeks following, the weather grew mild for North Dakota. With their own wedding on the horizon, there were many excuses for Ben to take extra trips to Bismarck, and while Rose (and on occasion, "Crazy Mary," as Ben called her mother) shopped for cloth goods for dresses, and for Rose's hope chest items, Ben had ample opportunity to conduct business and enjoy pleasure in Bismarck.

After the Christmas and Circumcision religious holidays, preparations for the wedding became the main focus of the Welsley household. The date was set: April 10, 1912, the Wednesday after Easter. The wedding was planned to take place before spring planting, and it would be a large affair at St. Mary's in Bismarck. Ben had nearly completed his Catechism studies and was ready for his "conversion" on Easter Sunday. However, facetiously he had misgivings about religious training. He pondered, Why in the world would anyone want to be like any of these so-called Christians? You have to hand it to them, they stick to their guns about not having too many vices during their so-called holy time, but it sure hurts my pocketbook. Fortunately, Mardi Gras would be coming soon. His new church friends planned to celebrate heavily before their long forty days of abstinence.

Rueben sat at his large oak desk in the back of the mercantile. He pulled out his gold watch, attached to a chain, from his vest pocket. The train should be rolling in any minute now, he thought. It's been four weeks since our pretentious Christmas engagement. Surely, that should be enough time for Rose to come to her senses. Any day now, a letter should arrive.

As the large black steam engine pulled into St. Giles, Rueben walked across the snow-packed dirt road to the train depot. He watched as the railroad man threw mail bags into the arms of the depot agent. As the postmaster of St. Giles, Rueben retrieved the bags. It was his job to sort letters into individual mailboxes, and then sort out the mail that needed to be delivered to neighboring farms. Sometimes, his rural postal carrier would deliver mail by auto, but more often, by horse.

Rueben shook the letters out of the heavy canvas bag. He instantly recognized the handwriting on a letter without a return address. He locked the front door of the store, turned the sign to "CLOSED," stepped into his office, and opened the letter.

My Dearest Rueben,

I must talk to you as soon as possible. I'm being haunted by an ongoing dream that I'm falling. In the dream, you've already fallen and you're lying lifeless at the bottom of Buffalo Jump. I think it's an omen. Anna says dreams have powerful meanings. Rueben, I believe we're both on paths to unintended destinies. I want you to know that I have strong feelings for you. I don't know what they are, but I know if I don't explore them, I will always be fearful that I made a terrible mistake. Mama is very sick and I cannot leave her side. I cannot visit you alone. Ben has always been suspicious of my feelings toward you, and I must be honest, if Ben knew I wrote this letter, I'm afraid he would kill me. Lillian has had enough pain, and if she loses you, I'm afraid for the course her life would take. You seem to have fallen completely in love with her, and I am happy for her, but something just doesn't appear natural. Ben and I are planning to attend the Saturday evening Mardi Gras dance that you're hosting, only four days before your wedding. I understand it will be a grand affair to celebrate your upcoming nuptials. Please wait for me.

Sincerely, Rose

Rueben let his head rest on the desk. He'd never prayed much before, but today he prayed a prayer of gratitude to whoever was listening.

He folded up the letter and put it on the inside pocket of his vest near his heart. As he rose to leave his office to unlock the front door to the store, he heard the swish of a skirt pass by his office door. Standing in the middle of the floor, Anna stared into his face. It was disconcerting, as if she could read his soul. She said nothing, and only turned and left through the side door, which he hadn't thought about locking. On the countertop, the glass display case was now full of beautifully decorated chocolates for the upcoming wedding. He wondered if Anna suspected something.

Mardi Gras could not arrive soon enough for the younger adults Ben, Rose, Rueben, Lillian, and Anton. The cows were getting close to calving. The days were getting longer and the sun's strength was increasing. While watching for early spring calves, and with the wintering gully so close to the still, Anton and Ben were able to get quite a large quantity of whiskey brewed for Mardi Gras, despite having to scrape dead rodents off the top of the mash. To escape the winter cold, the foul-smelling critters had dug themselves into the mash, where they bloated and died. Fortunately, there were no snakes to contend with. All of the reptiles had hibernated for the winter.

The large manure piles near the still had warmed enough to provide a medium for making a different, much more potent type of corn whiskey. Ben and Anton added the manure to their mash instead of lye to speed up fermentation.

Feeling confident they had enough alcohol for the upcoming party in St. Giles, the partners kept Big Red and his brothers personally supplied for hauling brew. The river was still frozen over, so transportation by horse proved easy. Finding places to hide the alcohol was even easier because of the customers Ben had made during Halloween and the winter holidays.

Rose gazed in the mirror. Ben had purchased a beautiful, green silk dress for her for to wear to the Mardi Gras dance. She loved the fabric, but the top was cut far too low, she felt, and showed an immodest amount of her décolletage. Why does Ben insist on dressing me like that woman Sally? Rose questioned. Sometimes, she appears out of nowhere and acts like she knows Ben like a long-lost friend. She took off the dress and hung it in her large armoire, eyeing other possibilities. She felt she should wear something more respectable, something Rueben may like, but she was pleased with her hair, still preferring to wear it long, and not in waves as was popular. Quickly, she put on a blue skirt with matching jacket over the top of a high-collared lace-trimmed blouse. She felt much more comfortable. Maybe she could tell Ben it was just too chilly this time of year for the green dress.

Ben dressed in the new suit he'd recently purchased in Bismarck. The shiny, silver-thread brocade vest over the tie and beneath the jacket created a strikingly different-looking man. He thought he resembled Anton's gambling friends. In his own opinion, he was dashing with his recently grown, handlebar mustache waxed and curled to tip upward on either side of his lip. Yes, quite a gentleman tonight. He couldn't wait to see Rose in that green dress.

While Ben waited impatiently for Rose to descend the stairs, Anton stood near the front door and rattled coins in his pocket. It sure shouldn't take Rose all this time to put on one simple dress.

Ben thought about his business, and remembered the Halloween near-disaster. He'd decided to pack his Smith and Wesson now to every event, because the lawmen were getting a little too wise, and Anton needed to be kept in line.

As Rose descended the stairs in her blue suit, Ben felt the blood rise up his neck. They had no time to waste, however, and so to avoid making a scene, Ben helped bundle up Rose into her coat so they could get going. He would address the issue of the dress later on; if Rose was going to be his wife, there would need to be some obedience. Wasn't that in the wedding vow?

This time of year, the narrowest and safest place to cross the river on ice was the Gwyther crossing south of the farm, which meant a seven-mile ride north to St. Giles on the other side of the river. Anton drove while Ben and Rose huddled in the back seat. They planned to stay at the boarding room-restaurant where Lillian worked part time. With the impending wedding, Rose didn't feel comfortable staying in Lillian's home, especially because of the letter Rose had sent to Rueben.

Outside the dance hall, Lillian dashed to the auto to embrace Rose before she even had a chance to step out. The friends rushed into the dance hall arm in arm to escape the cold air. Inside, Lillian said, "Look at the beautiful baked goods we made for this evening!" Anna stood near the platters of heart-shaped chocolates and other treats displayed on silver trays. "I made some chocolates just for you for Valentine's Day. See, they are rose-shaped and have just a small amount of sugar syrup filling. I know you love chocolates. Please try them."

Rose tested one of the chocolates. "Oh, these are heavenly, so smooth and creamy." Lillian laughed as Rose treated herself to several more. Lillian wandered off to greet other guests.

Rose wandered into the main part of the dance hall to find Ben and Anton, but they were nowhere to be seen. "Good evening," said a voice behind her. Chills ran up Rose's back. She turned to look into Rueben's eyes. She blushed.

"Rose, you look exceptionally beautiful tonight," Rueben said, eyes soft and kind. "May I add my name somewhere on your dance card?"

Rose knew she'd made the right decision in sending the letter to him. "Why, yes. I'd be delighted."

Ben entered the dance hall. Rose knew there would be trouble if he saw Rueben talking to her alone, and so she acknowledged Ben's presence. "Rueben and I were just discussing what a lovely winter day it is," she said, and felt Ben's strong hand grip her elbow. He said, "Let's go outside and enjoy it, then." He snatched her from Rueben's presence.

"How many times do I have to warn you about sneaking off to talk to him?" Ben growled into her ear.

"Let go of my arm. I accidentally bumped into him. He's getting married in a few days, you know. What are you so afraid of?" She wrinkled her nose. "Where have you been? What is that strong smell? Don't tell me you have been sipping with those roughnecks out back. I will not tolerate that in my own marriage." By standing up to him, she surprised even herself.

"Don't you worry about where I am or what I do," Ben said. He loosened his grip and softened his demeanor. "We came to have a good time. Let's dance." He pulled her toward the dance floor. "Rose, you may not feel this for me now, but I love you with all my heart. In time, I know that you will feel the same way. I'm going to make you happy, and I'm going to take you to see the world. I see how you look at pictures of Rome and the home of Pope Pius X in *National Geographic*. This week, the new steam liner, the Titanic, is taking passengers across the ocean. I am going to take you on that ship someday, Rose. I promise. I'm going to provide for you very well. You just have to be patient with me and not ask questions."

Rose stiffened as Ben pulled her close for a slow waltz. She looked past his shoulder to see if she could find Rueben.

Lillian hurried onto the dance floor and pulled Rueben along with her. A slow waltz, Rueben did not hold Lillian close. Instead, he held her at arm's length as they whirled around the room. As they circled the dance floor, Rueben looked for Rose, and when their eyes did meet, the words that passed between their glances didn't need to be spoken. Rueben seethed with loathing as he watched Ben nuzzle up against Rose's neck. Ben appeared to be talking, whispering in her ear. How he hated the man. Rueben discreetly tried to watch Ben. After a couple of dances, Ben left the dance hall, and Rueben quickly moved toward Rose. "I believe it's my turn for a dance," he suggested softy and took her hand. He wrapped his arm around her small waist. "I requested the band play a slow number so that we can talk." They danced without words for one round, and then Rueben spoke, "I knew you would write. We don't have much time until this song ends. Rose, it is either me or Ben. Meet me at the boarding house when you make your choice. I am now owner of that building, and I must check to be sure there is enough wood for the furnace for the night. When I see a lit candle in the kitchen window, I'll know you've made your choice to shine your light for me forever, giving up all. If you choose me, we can leave for South Dakota tonight; I have my auto packed and ready to go. When we cross the border, we can get married. In McLaughlin, a family friend is a justice of the peace and a well-known photographer. Frederick would be happy to marry us. I'll leave everything for you."

Ben shoved Rueben roughly aside. "Didn't I warn you to stay away from my gal? If I ever see you touch her again, you'll answer to my friends, Mr. Smith and Mr. Wesson."

Hearing the argument on the dance floor, Lillian ran to Rose's side. "These boys are always on each other's nerves. Are you feeling well? You look pale. Let's go next door and begin preparing food for the after-dance meal. It's best we let Ben and Rueben calm down."

"No, Lillian. This is your party. I will go next door and start the sausage and potatoes. Please, stay here and enjoy your other guests. I really need some air and space to be alone right now."

Lillian helped Rose put on her heavy, wool coat and walked her to the door. "Rose, everything will be all right in the morning. I promise."

Rose stepped into the cold, North Dakota winter's night. The night sky was clear, and Rose sent a prayer heavenward for St. Valentine, the patron saint of love. Light from the half-moon lit her footsteps.

A giggling couple bumped into her. They'd obviously been drinking. They could barely hold each other up. Where are they getting the alcohol? she wondered.

Once inside the kitchen, Rose sat at the table and painfully weighed her choices. She noticed an unlit candle in a brass holder sitting on the window sill, a box of farmer matches next to it. How could she choose? Rueben? Ben? Neither? Where had her dreams of teaching school vanished to? She stood up and started a fire in the cook stove. Looking in the sideboard, she found a large pot for cooking sausage. She added snow to a white, painted-enamel coffee pot to make fresh water to brew coffee. When she began to peel potatoes, a wave of despair came over her. She looked for a place to rest. On the main floor was a large bay window with a settee. Rose sat down. She unlaced and kicked off her shoes, and the hair on the back of her neck stood up. Why did she always feel as though she was being watched? Good heavens, was she going to inherit Mama's problems? Watching Mama go insane was beginning to rob her of compassion. Ben had suggested a hospital for her.

Exhausted, Rose lay on the settee. It seemed her life was about everyone else. Papa wanted her to marry to stay on the farm. Anton was the only one who wanted her to go to school to become a teacher, but his reasons were selfish. Ben wanted her to be someone she wasn't, more like Sally. Lillian, her best friend, was going to marry the man she recently recognized feelings for. Maybe life would be easier for everyone if she just weren't here.

Oh, dear God in Heaven, what should I do? She tried to sit up, but felt nauseated when she did. She had dozed off when Ben staggered into the room. He pounced on her and became roughly amorous, but Rose felt repulsed by the alcohol on his breath. He placed his hands where no decent man should, and she did her best to fight him off, but she was no match for his animal-like strength.

"C'mon, Rose," he said. "We're practically married. Quit being such a prude. Here, try this. It'll warm you up a bit." Ben took the flask and forced it into her mouth. Rose choked and tried to scream. The liquid seared as it went down the back of her throat. Ben allowed her to gulp for breath, but once again he forced the flask down her throat. The liquid scorched her. She felt helpless and he repeated the action until the flask was nearly empty. Feeling light-headed from the strong whiskey, Rose screamed. "So this is what you want? A drunken hussy? Well, then give me that bottle, and I will give her to you!" She grabbed the flask from Ben's hand and downed the rest. She grabbed Ben by the hair and forced his lips down on hers. Before she knew it, the intimate act she feared was over.

"Now, that's more like it," Ben slurred. He reassembled his pants and staggered out the door. "I'll be back with more. Don't go anywhere."

Rueben paced outside a safe distance from the kitchen window. He waited to see the lit candle. Impatient, he decided to look into the bay window to see if Rose was still there. He saw Ben and Rose seemingly lost in their lovemaking, and he knew all his dreams had been shattered.

Rueben put his back against the side of the house. He slid down to bury his face in his crossed arms. Cold air finally brought him to his senses and he decided to go to the kitchen for a cup of coffee.

Rueben peered into the parlor. Ben was gone. He walked into the room. Rose stirred on the couch, hair disheveled, her jacket thrown off, blouse torn. Good heavens, she was obviously intoxicated. "Rose, Rose," he whispered. "Here, drink some coffee. It's extra-strong, just for you."

"What happened?" Rose sniveled. She sipped the hot coffee, and set it aside. "Where am I? The room is spinning. I must lie down."

"You tell me," Rueben countered. He topped off her coffee. He put in a large scoop of sugar, the way she liked it.

Hurt and angry, he left the room. He walked back to the dance hall, and decided to tell Lillian the façade was over.

Anna rushed into the dance hall. "Come quickly!" she said. "I found Rose. She has a terrible headache and upset stomach. She tried to walk, but couldn't. Anton helped me carry her to the bedroom. She complained of being stiff and lame all over. Anton said he would take care of her."

Lillian and Rueben followed Anna to the boarding house. Inside the bedroom, Rueben looked down at Rose lying on the bed. Her hair was undone and spread around her face like a sleeping princess. She lay very still, face flushed. From a dark corner, Anton spoke. "She's dead."

The Death Probe
1912

Rueben ran to the mercantile to get his gun. He figured Ben must have given Rose rotgut alcohol, and it killed her.

Rueben pulled his shotgun from behind a store shelf. He loaded it and placed extra shells into his vest pocket. He marched to the dance hall and gathered a makeshift posse to hunt down Ben. They spread out, and soon the area was crawling with men ready to employ vigilante justice, but Ben had long vanished into the night. Rueben had underestimated Ben's horsemanship skills and his ability to disappear.

Still under the influence of his own brew, and believing he was being pursued by revenuers, Ben fled bareback on Lillian's horse into the night. The stallion galloped as fast as he could make it go. Ben hung onto its mane and hoped the animal would be surefooted. When he was safely out of sight, he could deal with his thoughts about what happened with Rose, but for now, survival was the only thing that mattered.

Anna thought it best not to get involved. She covered the face of young Rose and left her with Anton. Outside in the cold air, an auto nearly missed her. She thought, These people don't have anything more to fear from the Indian. They are their own enemy now with their greed and drink. She had seen the owl earlier in the evening, and she knew death and evil would follow. She considered fetching Fr. Logan for Rose, but decided against it. She was done with the confusion. She would go back to her own ways.

Automobiles and horses went in every direction in search of Ben. From the public pay phone recently installed in the mercantile, Rueben called the Morton County sheriff.

In the early morning hours, the sheriff and a perturbed Justice Gertenhem arrived at the boarding house. Because the chief coroner was out of town, the deputy coroner was summoned to the house. The consensus of the lawmen was that Anton was not a suspect, even though he had been the last person to see Rose alive; after all, he was her brother. He was told to return home to inform his parents.

The sheriff questioned Rueben. "Can you tell me how you knew Miss Welsley?"

"Rose and I were school friends. She was my fiancée's best friend."

"Do you know of any reason someone would want to harm Miss Welsley?"

"Absolutely not! Rose was a wonderful, sweet woman. She wanted only to be a schoolteacher, but she was engaged to someone incorrigible and possibly corrupt. Ben Hofts."

The sheriff eyed Rueben. "Don't leave this area until we summon an inquest jury. I have the deputy out gathering up farmers right now."

Rueben found Lillian in the kitchen tidying up. She was busy washing dishes, pots, and pans as though nothing had happened.

"Lillian, did you have anything to do with this? All I need is some scandal."

Lillian stopped scrubbing. "Of course I had nothing to do with this. Rose was my best friend. I loved her." She continued washing. "Please, go up the hill and get Fr. Logan."

Fr. Logan walked into the bedroom and uncovered Rose's face. "Dear God, what happened here? Don't tell me Rose has taken drink! Why are her clothes torn? What happened to her? Who did this?" The priest inspected her body. "She is in no condition for last rites!" He made the sign of the cross over her face, and then carefully covered her with the blanket. He turned to Rueben, and said, "I will deal with the death after the lawmen have finished their work."

Tables and chairs were set up in the dance hall for the inquest. The deputy had assembled twelve farmers. They decided that because there were no physical injuries, and because Miss Welsley was a beloved member in communities on both sides of the river, that her death must have been from natural causes. She did have alcohol on her breath, but she had been at a dance with lively dancers. It was not uncommon for young people to find a bootlegger at one of these events. She was pronounced dead of a heart attack, and they ordered her body be taken to Gwyther to await shipment to Bismarck by train Tuesday evening. This would give the sheriff time to finish the investigation. In Gwyther, they placed the body into a make-shift morgue behind Weads's store on Main Street.

Chris and Mary Welsley arrived at the west-side river community of Gwyther late Sunday morning. Still in disbelief and in shock from Anton's frantic message earlier that morning, they were grateful they could still cross the river by ice in the Model T. Together with Anton, they entered the makeshift morgue where Rose lay covered with a quilt on a table in the back of the grocery store. Chris held Mary around the shoulders as they looked at the body of their daughter. Mary opened her mouth to scream, but nothing came out, and she shook uncontrollably and fell to the floor into a fetal position. The deputy attempted to help Chris and Anton lift Mary to her feet, but she exhibited abnormal strength, and the men couldn't control her as she clawed, bit, and did everything in her power to attack them. With the help of the sheriff, they finally subdued her, and they were forced to tie her up. The sheriff informed Chris that she'd gone mad. He'd seen this happen before, he said, and there was no choice but to take her directly to the North Dakota Hospital for the Insane. Normally, a trial would be held in front of an insanity board, but it was obvious that Mary had lost all control of her mind. Chris felt numb.

Trying to ignore his throbbing head, Anton stood silently behind his father and watched Chris sink to the floor near to his beloved daughter's body. Nervous, Anton rattled a few coins in his pocket and thought about an unfinished game of cards back in St. Giles. Maybe he did love his sister, in his own way, but he knew that this was the day of his inheritance, which was rightfully his. Anton removed his hat from his head. He held it across his chest as his father grieved. He rocked nervously from one foot to the next, and he determined that he must be the hero in all this. He could prove to his father that he was worthy of the farm. He would find the killer, and he knew where to begin his search.

After a long night of chaos, and after she had attended Sunday morning Mass, Lillian convinced Rueben to drive Fr. Logan to Gwyther. She couldn't bring herself to the confessional—not yet.

As they drove southward on the gray winter's day, Lillian engaged the young priest in conversation. Rueben glanced her way several times as if to show he was perplexed by all her questions. "Fr. Logan," she asked. "Will the person who murdered Rose go to Hell?"

"Yes, the person who murdered Rose will go to Hell, unless they make a proper confession and penance before they die."

"Will that person, after they commit a murder and make a proper confession and do their penance, have to spend time in Purgatory?"

"Yes, possibly. There are many ways to shorten the time spent there. One can earn indulgences, for instance, by working for the church, or by saying certain prayers. Purgatory is meant to purge one's soul of any sin it may have still carried at the time of death. A soul will want to be in Purgatory; it will know that it's not good enough to go to Heaven."

Lillian pressed further. "What is the punishment in Purgatory? Is it painful?"

"Yes, it will be painful, but not like physical pain. The soul will feel guilty, regretful, grieved, and selfish. It will feel all the misery it caused others in this life."

Rueben remained silent as he drove along and listened to the conversation. He knew from his Protestant background that everything they were discussing was all hogwash. He just didn't know enough to argue. "Lillian, why all the questions?" he interrupted. "Let Fr. Logan prepare himself for meeting with the Welsleys when we get to Gwyther."

Further on, Fr. Logan continued the conversation. "Rueben, I understand you and Lillian plan to have a civil wedding ceremony. You do know that Lillian's marriage will not be recognized in the church. She may still receive the sacraments, but she will have to make a confession before she receives Holy Communion each day."

Rueben replied, "Right now, Fr. Logan, I would rather be in Hell. It can't be much worse than right here, except possibly somewhat warmer, and that would be a blessing."

Fr. Logan decided now was not the time to work on Rueben's conversion, but it would happen. He also knew something was not right with this young couple. Lillian's best friend, who had supported her through all the misery she had gone through during the last two years, had just died. Where was Lillian's grief? What was the problem with Rueben, the loving, future husband? He seems harsh with his future bride of only a few days. Something was amiss. He would try to talk some sense into Lillian before she marries Rueben without the church's blessing, but there would be time for that later. First, he was going to do his pastoral duty and call on the Welsley family before the body was sent up to Bismarck for the funeral service and burial. He was relieved to know that it wasn't going to be his parish's responsibility to perform the service. It didn't appear Rose was in a state of grace when she died. How does one tell the grieving parents of an upstanding church family that their daughter will not be allowed a Requiem Mass?

Anton's Revenge
1912

A lthough the sheriff and deputy concluded that Rose's death was the unfortunate, early demise of a promising young woman, Chris had his doubts. He was so wrapped up in his grief over losing Rose and then Mary, he'd forgotten about Ben. Why wouldn't the future husband of his daughter be here? He turned to Anton, "Where is Ben?"

"Be danged if I know," Anton answered, "but let me tell you somethin' about Ben: He's a rotten, good-for-nuthin', bootleggin', double-crossin' blackmailer. That's who he is, and Ben ain't even his real name. His real name is Clancy Coles, but he disguised himself real good."

"And just how do you know all this?" Chris demanded.

Anton looked sideways at the deputy coroner, and then answered. "I saw him giving Rose alcohol after the dance," he said. "They've been squabbling a lot lately, and I think he murdered her. I can't believe you were so blind to his bootlegging; he made whiskey right under your nose and using your own corn. You were completely hoodwinked by his plans for the farm and Rose. Revenuers are looking all over for him, and they say he murdered one of his own runners, a twelve-year-old boy, for double-crossing him."

The deputy coroner interrupted. "That fellow was in cahoots with that Mandan commissioner, Simon Gallack. They were running a blind pig operation out of a barbershop in Carson. They found a trap door under the barber chair and found a cave under the building. There were over a thousand bottles of whiskey in there and a complete gambling set up. They were catering to the railroad men over there. They found the Commissioner guilty, but they never could catch up with Clancy."

Anton became jumpy. He knew about that little gambling room, and he figured it was time to find an excuse to take his leave. Just then, Lillian, Rueben, and Fr. Logan arrived. They offered condolences to Chris, and Anton excused himself. He said he would try to find Ben.

It didn't take long. Anton had a good idea where Ben would be hiding out. After hitching a ride across the river at Gwyther, Anton hiked the rest of the way to the still. He noticed Lillian's horse tied up to a tree, and he knew that Ben—Clancy—was hiding out there.

"Clancy, you best stay under cover for a couple days," Anton shouted. "The whole area is crawling with revenuers. They're looking for the man who supplied the liquor last night. I don't know whether to thank you or kill you."

Clancy stepped out from behind the ramshackle shed that housed the still. He reached for his pistol, cocked the lever, and pointed it at Anton. "Get busy, and help me pack this up," he said. "It's time to move on. Put everything in these saddle bags."

With his free hand, Clancy dismantled the important parts of the still, careful not to bend the copper coils. Out of the corner of his eye, Anton spied the large paddle used for stirring mash. Seeing how Clancy was engrossed in his task, Anton grabbed the paddle and with one swift move, knocked him out.

Anton checked for a pulse. Clancy bled profusely and gagged up blood. He lifted his hand to recover his pistol, but Anton stepped on his wrist. Anton looked Clancy in the face and spat, "Have a good time in Hell, Catechism boy," and gave him a hard kick in the head to finish the job.

Anton flipped Clancy's body over the back of Lillian's horse. He led the horse to carry the lifeless cadaver to a large manure pile, where he buried the body. It was an appropriate grave, Anton figured, and besides, he couldn't dig a hole in the ground—it was still frozen. It would be a long time, if ever, before someone would discover the body, and in spring, the smell of the manure would mask the stench of rotting flesh. Clancy might never be found, or some hungry coyote might carry off his remains. Satisfied with his revenge, Anton felt a celebration was in order: He found the hidden whiskey and then wandered in the direction of the farmhouse to find Mama's church money.

Friends at Rest
1912

Chris looked at his watch. He hoped his unreliable son had used his common sense to complete the necessary chores at the farm, especially what needed to be done for the animals. He also hoped that Ben had gone back to the farm, too, to take care of the chores, and that Anton would bring him back to Gwyther before the train departed for Bismarck carrying Rose's body. Because the handmade coffin was too large to get into a motor vehicle, and because the coroner had his hearse out on official duty in another state, the only means of transporting Rose's body to Bismarck was by train. Chris wouldn't allow his daughter to be brought to Bismarck in an open wagon through the towns of St. Giles, Schmidt, and Mandan for all curiosity seekers to stare at. He paced around Gwyther on wooden sidewalks in the cold air, and he watched for any sign of Anton or Ben. He did not want to believe that Ben was actually a wanted man. He would not blame Ben unless there was proof. Chris had seen how Ben had loved Rose, and he saw how Ben treated the animals on the farm with kindness. He brushed off the idea that Ben could be a murderer. Finally, he gave up, and decided to drive his vehicle back to the farm across the ice.

Chris dreaded the thought of going to Rose's room to retrieve her burial dress. He should have asked Lillian for help while she was at the vigil, because he wasn't sure what items a young woman should wear with a dress. He'd have to remember her rosary, too, and baptismal candle, as well as her prayer book. He knew they would intertwine the rosary into her fingers, and the thought of this made him consider Lillian. Something seemed odd about her at the vigil because she insisted Rose should wear the engagement ring Ben had given her as a sign of their everlasting love. Wouldn't that be something Ben should request? He later noticed the ring had gone missing, and it struck him strange that Rueben and Lillian should be acting like two pole cats, hissing and whispering at one another while hovering near the body. Who can understand these young people nowadays? Fr. Logan had acted out of the ordinary, as well. He said very few prayers for Rose's soul, but maybe Fr. Logan knew his precious daughter only needed few, as pure as she was.

Overcome by the events of the last couple of days, Chris stopped the car in the middle of the frozen river. He laid his head into his hands and sobbed, and there was no one for miles to see him in his grief. Soon, long shadows from the riverbank darkened his path in the setting sun. With one last shudder, he rubbed his stinging eyes, and felt the rawness of his cheeks. He took a deep breath of cold air and drove slowly toward the east bank.

Chris had made the decision to hold the funeral service at the home of his brother-in-law in Bismarck. Due to unresolved questions surrounding Rose's death, he didn't want a large, public funeral, and he also didn't want embalming. Chris made arrangements for two Bismarck physicians to examine Rose's body when it arrived.

When the porters carried the plain, wooden coffin from the boxcar, Chris was surprised to see Rueben following behind. "I just felt it was the honorable thing to do, to accompany Rose on her last trip to Bismarck," Rueben said. "I always held Rose in high regard. In fact, I always hoped we could have been more than friends. I feel it necessary to get this off my chest: I can't help but wonder if things would have been different today if we could have just gotten past some of the ridiculous religious and social barriers that stood in the way of true love. I want to extend my deepest sympathy to you and your family." With that, Rueben covered his head with his hat, bent down to kiss the coffin, and walked off across the street toward the Hotel McKenzie to spend the night before the funeral.

Lillian paced the floor of her house. Today was Valentine's Day, the day of her wedding, but Rueben's car was not in front of the mercantile, nor in the shed, where he normally kept it.

Today was also Rose's funeral.

Lillian fumed. That's where he is. He went to Rose's funeral. He had to give one last farewell to his secret love. Even now, when Rose is dead, Rueben still puts her before me.

Remembering it was also Ash Wednesday, Lillian decided that she best not break any more church laws, and so she dressed for Mass in a black skirt and white blouse, and covered her head with a black scarf. She stared into the mirror. This was supposed to be the happiest day of her life.

Lillian walked up the hill and paused to look down at the growing little town. She counted the buildings she and Rueben would own. There would be the mercantile, boarding house, dance hall, and grain elevator, in addition to her small house. All this property in town, and she was barely nineteen years old. If she and Rueben were to marry today, she would be the most respectable woman around, and her parents could no longer say that she hadn't done well. The only thing missing would be genuine love from Rueben.

She turned and walked into the wood-frame church and knelt in the front pew. She pulled out her rosary and began reciting the Sorrowful Mysteries. She wondered how many times this would be necessary for a suffering soul. Lillian heard Fr. Logan open the creaky door on his side of the confessional; she wanted to be first today before other church members began to arrive. She stood up, walked to the confessional, pushed aside the heavy velvet curtain, and knelt down on the hard kneeler. She took a deep breath, and bowed her head. She began, "Forgive me Father, for I have sinned."

While Mary Welsley lay in a catatonic state in the State Hospital for the Insane, Chris helped to place Rose's coffin in the center of the large parlor at his brother-in-law's house. Mary's condition and the distance made attending the funeral impossible.

Two physicians from St. Alexius Hospital had examined the body, and they determined that without an autopsy, there was nothing more they could add to the police report. Because the body hadn't been embalmed, they recommended the body be buried quickly. The priest from St. Mary's would preside over the funeral service.

Soon, the small parlor filled with family, school friends, and neighbors. There were several rosaries said and stories shared, and as the pallbearers lifted the coffin into a black-draped wagon led by a team of horses, Chris looked through the crowd hoping that Ben may have decided to attend the funeral. Still not believing the story he was sure Anton had concocted, he walked through the crowd that had gathered outside the house. There he saw Anton speaking with a couple of men, who rapidly wrote notes on paper tablets. When they saw Chris approach, they started to compete with each other and directed questions toward him.

"Are you Chris Welsley? Do you think your daughter was murdered? Who do you think killed your daughter? She had a beau, didn't she? Do you think he killed her in a fit of jealous rage? You would think a beau would be at his future bride's funeral, wouldn't you?"

Chris told Anton to get rid of the reporters. He wondered what Anton had already told them.

The funeral procession wound its way to St. Mary's Cemetery. There, high on the crest of the hill, Chris laid his young daughter to rest. The priest walked around the grave with the censor, praying in Latin, but Chris barely heard a word of it. He was wrapped up in the questions the reporters had asked him.

After everyone had left the hillside, one lone figure stood by the grave, tears streaking down his face. Rueben dropped a handful of dirt onto the grave and promised to visit. He looked up at the iron scroll cross that held an effigy of Jesus in the center. It had been crafted by one of Chris Welsley's neighbors, and Rueben had paid the blacksmith extra to add roses to the ironwork. He bowed his head and asked someone, anyone, to watch over her soul.

Lillian wandered slowly into the cemetery and stood at the foot of Josef's grave. She then moved to the gate and circled the fence to the grave of little Adam. After she prayed, she noticed Anna walking down the road toward her house. She rushed down the hill. She wanted to spend time with the only person she felt truly understood her.

Lillian invited Anna into the kitchen for a cup of tea. They sat in silence for some time, and then Anna spoke. "Have you made peace with the Great Spirit?" she asked. "You have troubles. There are two sides to every person, evil and good, but I think you know that. Your good and evil sides, they fight against each other. The medicines that I taught you, they have a good and evil side, too. I meant for them to be used for good, but I will not talk of this again. I'll leave you something: When Rueben returns, and I know he will, mix this in his tea. It is good medicine."

Across Smokey Waters
1912

Chris sat at the kitchen table with a cup of coffee. He felt immobilized. It was time for spring field work, but he had no desire to start planting. The overcast day added to his melancholy. He rubbed his forehead with his fingers and thought, There's nothing here to live for anymore. Anton was gone most of the time, sometimes for days, and more than likely, he was up to something illegal. Mary lay curled up into a ball at the State Hospital, and Rose was dead. The only thing that gave him any purpose for living was the murder investigation.

Every day, Chris begged, "Please, God, before I die, I want revenge for my little girl. Help the law find the killer and bring whoever it was to justice." There were so many unanswered questions, including, Where was Ben? And why hadn't Lillian showed up for the funeral? Chris remembered calling on Lillian at the mercantile. He'd offered to give Rose's personal things to her, but she refused to take them. Oddly, Rueben contacted him later and said he knew of a good charity that could use Rose's belongings and he offered to pick up the items. Meanwhile, Chris had hired Anna to keep the house and cook for the hired men, but she was an odd one, and not much for company. She barely spoke more than ten words at a time and she insisted on sleeping in the attic instead of Rose's bedroom.

Chris drank the last of his coffee. He spoke aloud, "Well, I best be getting down to the cattle in the draw."

Anna watched Chris walk in the direction of the cattle pens. She was happy now to have moved to this side of the Smokey Waters, her people's name for the river. There was too much evil on the hill side of the river; the white priest had desecrated her people's sacred land. Before she left, she felt obliged to cleanse that place, and when the church building burned, it went down so quickly, no one could save it.

Anna had noticed pheasants around the farmyard this morning. The pheasant is a warning; something has been concealed in this place.

For Chris, there was nothing more calming than watching young calves buck and play in the morning sun, which had finally broken through the clouds, and for a moment, he felt a ray of hope. Warm spring weather had caused the piles of manure to thaw, and while some folks couldn't stand the stench of thawing manure, to Chris it was the smell of prosperity. His Indian farm hands had begun to move the excess out to the field for fertilizer, and he saw one of the young men stop loading the manure into a wagon and begin to wave his arms wildly in the air. "Boss, Boss!" yelled the tall, lanky Indian. "Come here!"

Chris bolted toward the frantic voice to see what the commotion was about. As he approached, the stench became appalling, and he had to put his handkerchief over his nose. His stomach turned. The Indian had found a partially decomposed human body in an unmistakable suit of clothes. It was Ben, and his head had been bashed in.

Chris knelt down on one knee. He made the sign of the cross and thanked God he hadn't been wrong about Ben. Obviously, whoever killed Rose had killed Ben, as well. Who would have wanted them dead?

Chris hurried to the farm house. He took the Model T from the shed and decided to drive to Bismarck to inform the sheriff. He felt it would be better if he explained what was found and where they could investigate.

Chris met the sheriff at the corner at the gate to the farmstead. "We're doing everything in our power to find who did this," said the sheriff. "We'll consider you next-of-kin, and we'll release his body to you; it's far too decomposed to get any clues as to who may be responsible."

Chris and his farm hands wrapped the remains in a blanket. He built a rectangular, wooden box for a coffin. He'd considered cremating the body, but that wouldn't have been allowed in his Catholic beliefs, and because Ben hadn't been baptized, there would be no funeral Mass, but the priest in Bismarck gave Chris permission to bury Ben in St. Giles alongside the un-baptized babies outside the cemetery fence. Chris took time to visit the new granite works in Bismarck and ordered a headstone for Ben. Together, Chris and the hired men found Old Joe and transported the body to St. Giles on the raft, and then quietly, they buried the body. At day's end and with heavy hearts, the group of men watched the sun send streaks of gold, blue, and purple across the western sky. With only minutes of daylight left, the small group hurried back to the east side of the river.

After a long weekend in Bismarck, Anton asked Anna where his father had been all day. She didn't answer, so he went to his parent's bedroom to search for hidden cash. He knew all the places they used to hide money for emergencies or until they could get to First National Bank in Bismarck. Anton had more important things to do than help with spring planting.

Although he hadn't legally inherited the farm, Anton had lost all future rights in a game on Saturday night. He thought he could keep up with those boys from Chicago, but the only problem was, they wanted payment now, so he needed cash to keep them off his back until he could win it all back.

Anton frantically rummaged around the bedroom until he found the deed to the farm tucked into the family Bible. He slid it into his vest pocket and then rushed from the house. He'd agreed to meet the collectors south of Bismarck at the town of Glencoe at sundown on Sunday, and he knew they meant business. He made the tired mare gallop at full speed until he reached the cemetery near the church, where two well-dressed men waited in a shiny new, black automobile. Anton never felt the sting of the bullet as it entered the back of his head.

On Monday morning, Anna saw an owl circle overhead, and then she saw the sheriff approach. He knocked on the door to the house and peered in the window. He knocked again. Anna didn't answer. She kept busy.

When he heard the urgent knocking, Chris stood up from the table and quickly walked to the door. "Hello Sheriff," he said. "What brings you all the way out here so early in the morning?" He hoped to hear good news about the murder investigation, and closed the door as he stepped outside.

After a long conversation, Anna watched through the window as the sheriff shook Chris's hand and patted him on the shoulder. The sheriff got back into his car and drove slowly out of the yard.

Anna knew she wouldn't be able to stop him, so she watched helplessly as Chris took his shotgun from the wall. He slowly wandered to the barn, and Anna stiffened when she heard the blast. Once again, she stepped outside to mourn in Lakota.

Anna Returns to St. Giles
1930

Lillian stood at the sink washing dishes. She looked up and out her kitchen window when she froze. Good heavens! She must be hallucinating! Down the road toward the house walked a familiar figure. It was Anna.

After Chris Welsley had died, Anna disappeared, and she left her home to the coyotes. Lillian had inquired about her in Ft. Yates, but Anna's relatives wouldn't reveal her whereabouts. It had been eighteen years now since Lillian had last seen the Lakota woman, but there was no mistaking the apparition that came closer to her house.

Lillian's heart raced. Anna was the only person alive who knew the truth about how Rose died. Why is she here? Had she come for revenge?

Anna rounded the house. The inevitable knock came at the door. "Anna! How wonderful to see you!" Lillian said. "Where have you been all these years? I have been trying to get in contact with you!" Lillian tried to embrace her old friend, but felt no arms return the gesture. It was as if she had embraced a tree trunk.

Lillian held Anna at arm's length and looked into her eyes. They were expressionless. She released her hold on Anna's arms, and felt cold emanating from her friend. "Anna, I have so much to tell you," Lillian said. "You were my only real friend in the world. Please, come inside. We can talk until Rueben comes home from the grain elevator. Such trouble, all is nearly lost."

Anna stepped inside the house and looked around. "Lillian, you know why I left. There was too much evil here, and someone needed to take care of Mr. Welsley. I came back to sell my property. I thought I would look around to see if anything had changed."

Lillian started to feel a sense of relief. Maybe Anna would sell her place and move on. She shuddered to think about what Anna knew.

Anna continued, "I see you're still married to Rueben. You've built a fine home. I don't see any children."

The comment stung. Of course there were no children. How could there be? There must be love between a man and woman to create a child. Lillian's marriage to Rueben was far from love. They had grown comfortable, more like roommates, but Lillian was satisfied. She'd gained respect in the community, and her parents invited her back into the family after Rueben's confirmation in the Catholic Church. Until the stock market crashed, they'd lived well, and she'd created a beautiful garden. She had important daily duties at the church, which had been rebuilt after the fire. Rueben spent much of his time in Bismarck arranging business deals and hobnobbing with political friends.

"No, Anna," Lillian said. "Rueben and I never had any children."

Anna sighed. "I tried to help you, Lillian. I really did."

Anna stepped out of Lillian's home and closed the door silently behind her. She'd lived with a restless conscience long enough and planned to make peace with her old friend, but she knew she'd have to tread lightly. She feared all the evil of so long ago, but she wanted to teach Lillian how to free her spirit. She wanted to convince Lillian to tell the truth. Because of all the things she'd taught Lillian, Anna felt responsible. Perhaps she'd taught her too much.

Anna was near to the end of her time on the earth, and she knew it. No medicine could stop her illness.

The following morning started out hot and windy. Lillian woke up early to walk to Anna's crumbling home to see if she needed help with cleaning, and to keep a close eye on her. Walking along the gravel road, Lillian admired the wild sunflowers that grew along the way. She was amazed they could grow in this drought. When she neared Anna's house, she saw smoke rising from a fire burning in the yard. Worried it may have been accidental, Lillian picked up her pace to see if everything was all right. "Anna! What's burning? We have to put this fire out; it could start a prairie fire in this drought."

"Nothing for you to worry about," Anna answered. She tossed paper after paper into the flames.

Lillian looked at the papers strewn about the pile. She recognized them as recipes for medicines. "Don't worry, Anna. I have all the recipes you wrote out for me. The good and the bad medicines, I have them all. They were all your creations. I knew nothing about native remedies. I was only your student."

Lillian turned away and strode back toward her house. She knew something had to be done. Anna would never live with injustice, and Lillian was positive that the Lakota woman would go to the authorities.

It had been 18 years since Rose died, but whenever there was a dance in St. Giles, it seemed as though some of the conversations were accusatory. The subject would quickly change if she drew near, or was it her own conscience that she heard? Surely, by now her debt to God had been paid, what with all the improvements to the church and the extra gifts to the diocese.

When Lillian returned home, Rueben was sitting at the dining room table with a large stack of papers. He swore under his breath as he shuffled through them. It was harvest, and the grain elevator should be full, but the drought had left local farmers with very little crop, and there were only a couple of loads there. The farmers had immediately taken what they harvested to Mandan to sell. "Dang it all, Lillian, we are over our heads in debt. I am going to have to do something drastic to dig out of this hole. I've decided to sell the dance hall and to try to get something going with politics. My father says he and the boys at the lodge will see to it I get a seat. If I win, I may have to move to Bismarck during the legislative session, which means you'll have to stay here and run the mercantile and the grain elevator, but you can handle it. It will be for just a few months every year."

Lillian hadn't felt this level of anxiety in eighteen years. She went to her sanctuary, a small storage room in the basement, where she kept her mementos of the past. She plopped down on a large trunk and reached behind it to retrieve a bottle of gin. She opened the cover and poured the burning liquid down her throat. After another large drink, she would begin to relax. She just had to think. She needed a plan.

Shuffling through her papers, she came across the insurance policies. She found one for the grain elevator worth ten thousand dollars. Rueben had purchased many insurance policies from his father's friends. She thought, Anna, fire, accident, insurance; it would work. Another deep gulp of gin and she made her way to her bedroom to pray her rosary.

The following day was hot and dusty. Lillian noticed Anna walking up the road toward the cemetery on the hill. "Anna, where are you going?" Lillian called. "Can I walk with you for a bit?"

"I am going to pay my final respects to my neighbors who went to the spirit world when I was away," Anna said. "I would prefer to be alone when I pray."

Lillian's eyes followed Anna up the hill. She realized that her old friend was aging and not as strong as she used to be. In fact, she didn't look well. For a moment, she almost felt sad.

Lillian waited for Anna to come back from the cemetery. She sat on her garden bench and looked at the grain elevator. It was the tallest structure for miles. As Anna made her way slowly down the hill toward the main road in St. Giles, it appeared as though she were struggling to walk. Could she be that ill? The right thing to do was to help. Lillian fingered the matches in her pocket.

When Lillian put her arm around Anna's small waist to help her walk, the old woman didn't resist. Lillian led her toward the grain elevator. They both looked at the sky to see an owl circle above. "Anna, I don't believe the grain elevator was built before you left," she said. "Let me show you inside." Lillian helped Anna over the stoop of the door into the empty office and then into the tall storage area. As the women looked up into the tall, empty chamber, dust danced like fairies in the sunlight that beamed in from high windows. "Anna, I know you're going to go to the authorities with the truth, but I can't let you do that. You'll destroy Rueben and me." She kicked a gas can toward Anna and the liquid streamed onto the floor. "See, this is how it will look: You came back to destroy this town. People around here remember who you are; they're still suspicious of the fire that burned down the church. Everyone in town knew you hated Fr. Logan, and it's no secret you despise Rueben." Anna's eyes begged for mercy as Lillian struck a match against the door post. Oh God, not again. Lillian held her hands over her ears as Anna sang her sad mourning song. It was the same Lakota song she had sung when Adam died.

Lillian backed out of the elevator and dashed across the road to her house. There was a loud explosion, and turning back to look, Lillian stared in disbelief at the inferno. She realized she could have been killed along with Anna.

Rueben charged out of the mercantile. He watched as the grain elevator went up in flames, and he knew it was hopeless to try to save. With the dry conditions and the intense fire, it was more important to put out the grass fire around it. Men, women, and children from all over town dug fire lines and formed bucket brigades to stop the inferno, but there was nothing left but ashes and the cement foundation.

Lillian ran to Rueben's side. "Rueben, thank God you had this insured!"

"Insured, my foot!" Rueben yelled. "I couldn't afford the premiums anymore, so I dropped the insurance a year ago!" Rueben crumpled to the ground and held his side.

"Rueben, Rueben! What happened? What's wrong?"

"I, I don't know... I see two of everything. Help..." Rueben whispered hoarsely as he blacked out.

The day after the fire, the inspector from Mandan came to St. Giles. Rueben was asleep in his bedroom, unable to move, and he refused to travel to see the doctor. The inspector spoke to Lillian. "It appears as though the fire was not an accident," he said. "We found a gas can in the ashes, as well as the bones of a human body. There were also silver jewelry items and a couple arrowheads."

"Oh, my Lord in Heaven!" Lillian said, as shocked as possible.

"Mrs. Muester, do you know who may have done this?"

Lillian pretended to go into a frenzy. "Yes, I think I do. Anna Crow Wing had just returned to St. Giles after being gone for eighteen years. She hated Rueben, and everything else about this town."

The inspector looked surprised. "I just talked to members of

Miss Crow Wing's family," he said. "They also thought it may have been she who was burned in the fire. She had become feeble-minded and wandered, and apparently was quite ill, possibly dying. She'd told them she came back to say goodbye to the little town and to the people she loved, especially you."

In the morning, a procession of Indians carried a small pottery jar of Anna's remains to the cemetery on the hill. They buried her remains outside the fence. They mourned in Lakota and beat drums. A man etched "Anna" into a field rock with a sharp knife and placed it on the grave.

Return to St. Giles
2012

It was a sweltering hot, summer day when Catherine returned to St. Giles. Whenever she returned for a visit, the memories of her childhood came rushing back. As she looked around the yard between the rundown mercantile and the weather-beaten house where Auntie had lived, she was saddened at how badly the buildings had fallen into disrepair. "Much like my own life," she muttered. An abusive husband. The looming divorce. Financial problems. The death of Daddy. It all weighed heavier than the high humidity against her skin. She'd been given anti-anxiety medications by her psychiatrist, but they only seemed to make her feel like she was in a fog. She'd decided to quit taking them weeks ago.

The cement foundation was the only visible evidence for where the grain elevator once stood. Catherine balanced on it like she used to when she was a kid. She used to pretend she was in the circus and balancing on a high wire. She jumped down from the foundation. She tried to remember her former neighbor's names, and where their houses once stood. Their homes had been torn down or moved away. Only a few buildings remained.

Catherine had come back to St. Giles to go through Momma's belongings. It had been an awful experience to move Momma to a nursing home, and she knew that sifting and sorting through fifty-plus years of her parents' belongings was going to be heart-wrenching, not to mention time-consuming. Momma was a saver and never threw away much, and Catherine supposed it was because she'd known hard times growing up after the Great Depression and the following war.

However, before Catherine would begin her task, she wanted to make a visit to the cemetery. She tried skipping up the small hill toward the church like she used to, but she ran out of breath halfway up. She admired the stone-and-cement church that had stood so many years, and she recalled attending Mass there nearly every day with Auntie. The stone church had been built to replace the wood-framed church that burned down.

Catherine kicked up small clouds of dust as she walked through the cemetery gate. She found Daddy's gravestone and sat with her back against the warm, granite marker. She noticed the graves of Josef, Auntie, and Rueben across the way, and she spied a couple of the small knolls that had been found to be Indian burial mounds. She looked toward the row of un-baptized baby graves, where baby Adam and many others were so carefully placed so as not to be on "consecrated" ground, which was reserved only for baptized Catholics.

She pulled herself up, and wandered along the row of un-baptized babies. She came across a square grave marker partially buried in the weeds, one she had never noticed before. The inscription was very strange: "Ben Hofts, Lost Feb, Buried April. 26 Years Old. Nothing Hidden, But Will Be Made Known." Catherine wondered why that person had been buried in a row reserved for babies.

Catherine stood next to Auntie's grave, and she looked out over the Missouri River. From the hill where the cemetery stood, she could see the farmstead where Rose and her family had lived.

She strolled down the hill, past the dilapidated dance hall into Auntie's yard. Daddy and Momma had bought Auntie's house after she passed away, and although Catherine herself had lived there for many years, it would always be known as Auntie's house. Lilac trees still surrounded the enclosed garden and the cottonwood trees had grown very tall.

Catherine decided it was best to get on with her task. She planned to start in the basement in the dark, damp storage rooms. When she spied a large trunk, she remembered the secret, and that Auntie would have something for her in this trunk, but the trunk was locked. Where was the key? It would be a large skeleton key.

She drove back to Bismarck. How could she have forgotten to keep her promise? In her apartment, she pulled out the storage box where she kept the yellowed envelope and the little Hummel that Auntie had given her. She'd packed the Hummel away many years ago for fear that her young children might break it. First, she opened the envelope and read the newspaper story about the death of Rose. The headline stood out in bold letters: "Mystery of Young Girl's Death to be Probed." Auntie had wanted her to reveal the real killer; she'd known all along, and said the answer would be locked in the trunk. It was the secret Catherine had to keep until long after Auntie's death, but Auntie had never told her where the key to the trunk had been kept.

Catherine carefully placed the newspaper story back into the crumbling envelope. She examined the Hummel, and read the inscription on the bottom: Luke 12:2. She found her Bible and looked up the verse: "For there is not anything secret that shall not be made manifest, or hidden that shall not be known." The verse sounded similar to the words on the strange grave marker at the cemetery. Could there be a connection?

Feeling she had a purpose, Catherine drove to the nursing home to see Momma. She had to ask her about the missing key to the trunk. She found her mother sitting in her wheelchair facing the window. "Hello, Momma, how did the Twins do today?"

"Not good. They were rotten last year, too, but someone has to go for the underdogs. How is all the sorting and cleaning going out at the house?"

"Momma, do you know where the big key for Auntie's trunk

might be kept? Did you and Daddy ever look inside?"

"Yes, we did, but only when Auntie was still alive. I'm sure it's just full of the same newspapers, pictures, and stuff that Auntie collected. We never felt the need to look in it again. I was just saving the old trunk in case one of you kids wanted it for something. I don't know where she kept the key, which was another reason why we never looked inside again. You know, Auntie was odd; she kept all kinds of things in strange places. We found cash and coins hidden in nooks and crannies all over the house. Look in the basement. All her prayer books and cookbooks are in a tin closet in the downstairs bedroom. I haven't gone down there in years because of my bad legs."

Catherine pushed Momma to the nursing home dining room and took in the scene. The nurse's aides pushed the residents up to the tables and fastened adult bibs around their necks. The old ones seemed pitiful and resigned to the fact that this was all there was going to be, their life's work was done, and now they were just biding their time until they were called. Some didn't appear to know that they were at the dinner table at all, and sat stooped over their plates playing with their food. What stories and secrets did these aged residents hold?

Catherine sat down with Momma. "I was walking around the cemetery today," she said, "and I saw a strange grave that appeared out of place. Did you know the Ben Hofts family? And why was he buried in the row of un-baptized babies?"

Momma slurped her soup as she tried to answer the question. "Nobody really knows who that is. The story is that he was murdered across the river and someone felt sorry for him and buried him up there. Perhaps they didn't know if he was Catholic or not, so they just put him over there." Momma picked at her tuna noodle casserole, and then threw down her fork "I can't eat this junk, Catherine. Take me home."

Her heart breaking, Catherine kissed her mother on the forehead and promised to take her for a ride to St. Giles on Sunday.

The Secret in the Trunk
2012

Catherine helped her Momma from the car. The matriarch's white cat, Casper, met her at the door and wound a circle-eight pattern around and between her legs. Fearful the purring feline might trip Momma, Catherine chased him down the steep basement steps.

With help, Momma settled into her favorite easy chair and then Catherine began the task of finding the trunk key. She thought about cutting the lock on the antique trunk, but decided to go through the tin closet in the spare bedroom first. With any luck, she would find the key there.

When she opened the closet, Catherine was amazed at all the scrapbooks filled with recipes for chocolates, jams, jellies, and baked goods, all handwritten in a beautiful cursive script. Another scrapbook contained notes regarding herbs, spices, teas, and elixirs, as well as records of the results people had experienced after using the recipes. Seeds and leaves were glued to the margins to show what the plants looked like.

Catherine carefully stacked the precious scrapbooks into plastic containers. They smelled musty. She then discovered a beautiful autograph book that belonged to Auntie. She sat down on a wood crate to read the many notes, and found an autograph from her grandmother, Daddy's mother. A wave of depression swept over her because when Catherine was a young girl, she'd often cried herself to sleep after overhearing stories whispered during late night conversations about how relatives of Auntie's family had shunned her for being pregnant before her marriage to Josef. Catherine had never seen her grandmother's handwriting before. She'd died before Catherine was born. The note was from 1904 and before all the problems started.

Next, Catherine read the inscription from Auntie's best friend, Rose Welsley:

Rivers Edge, No. Dak., December 25th, 1909
To Lillian,
When hills and rivers part us, and distance be our lot, dear Lillian,
forget me not.
Love, your friend forever. Rose Welsley

Catherine continued her search for the missing key. She rummaged through the middle shelf in the closet full of Catholic meditation, song, and prayer books. There were also Catechisms and books about the lives of saints.

She flipped through a prayer book. Prayers that offered the highest indulgences were marked 'memorize'. The old books were beginning to fall apart and smell musty.

Believing they were outdated, Catherine decided to place them into her recycle box. Finally, she found a very large, old Bible. She lifted it from the shelf and turned to the front inside cover, where Auntie had recorded her marriage to Josef, the death of Adam, and her family tree. She recorded her marriage to Uncle Rueben, and then sadly, there were no more baptisms recorded, except for Uncle Rueben's. He was baptized in 1912, around the time he married Auntie. What a surprise! He must have wanted to become a Catholic before they married.

Catherine flipped through the rest of the large Bible to find more personal notes. To her surprise, she found the antique skeleton key tucked into the binding and against a New Testament page with the verse Luke 12:2 underlined. It was the same verse noted on the Hummel, and similar to that strange inscription on the grave marker in the cemetery. Suddenly, the young, curious girl who lived within Catherine began to reappear. The young girl who'd loved a good mystery and became excited about someday solving one re-emerged.

Turning to head into the storage room, Catherine nearly stumbled over Casper. She picked up the white chunk of fur and took him upstairs to Momma. Momma slept soundly in her chair, so Catherine laid the kitty on her lap and backed out of the room. Momma's nap meant she'd have a couple of hours to dig in the trunk before having to take her back to the nursing home.

Catherine sorted through the photographs first, and she was astonished at how many Auntie had. She looked at a black-and-white photograph backed with hard cardboard and wondered who the young woman was who posed so seductively on the chair. Upon closer examination, she realized it was Auntie. The photo seemed to say, "I am unique. I am different." Catherine studied another photo of a very different young woman. She held a rose in her lap and was beautifully dressed in a high-collar blouse and black skirt. On the back of the photograph was a strange note: "Rose Welsley. Dead at eighteen." This must have been Auntie's best friend.

Catherine felt annoyed with herself. How could she have forgotten her promise for so long? Was her life that garbled that she would forget to do something so important? Were years of antidepressants and counseling messing up her mind? She remembered back to the day when Auntie told her about the large trunk where she stored her lifelong collection of newspaper stories, photographs, greeting cards, and other precious reminders of all her friends and relatives, and in that trunk would be a truth that she wanted revealed when she was long gone. She'd said something about her friend Anna telling her that only truth would set her spirit free. Later in the conversation, she'd said there would be a clue about Rose's death hidden somewhere among her personal items, but Catherine wasn't to look until fifty years had passed. She had to promise that when she found the clue, she would immediately reveal the truth to the proper authorities.

Catherine reached deeper into the trunk. Midway down, she came across a baby's blanket and bonnet. A note was attached to the blanket. It read, "For Baby's Baptism. Love, Godmother Rose." Carefully refolding the baby items, Catherine pulled out Auntie and Uncle Rueben's wedding photo. Apparently, men didn't smile on their wedding day then. Auntie smiled broadly, though, and even that expression was strange for a wedding photo from the time. All the other old photos of weddings showed a very somber bridal party.

Finally reaching the bottom, Catherine found more recipes, this time in a tin box, which had been tucked into the corner of the trunk. She opened the box and began reading. The recipes were for medicines, some written in German, while others were recorded using Indian pictographs. Among the recipes were native herbal remedies for everything from headaches to menstrual cramps, and in the back of the tin box were notes about herbs and plants not to be used. For example, water hemlock was not to be touched when searching for herbs along the river. Avoid touching the leaves of poison ivy and poison oak. Along with the notes were antidotes in case of accidental run-ins with one of the poisonous plants, and there were notes about poisonous insects and snakes, as well. Auntie appeared to have been a country doctor in her own right.

Catherine pulled out the last note in the box and read through it. The paper was a chokecherry jelly recipe, and she read the instructions while remembering it was one of her favorite jams on bread while growing up. Catherine wondered how difficult it would be to make. She flipped the paper over and read the back. She found a note that had been underlined. Catherine was taken aback.

Chokecherry Varmint Poison
Grind the very dry leaves, bark, and seeds of chokecherries to make a potent poison for rodents. The powder is best mixed with sugar to attract the animal.

An additional small note had been added to the card.

My dearest Catherine, you have found the secret. Yes, I killed Rose. Tell the world now by pen or by spoken word about how Rose died. I also killed Josef and Anna. They all deserved to die. I put Josef out of his misery, which ended my own misery, as well. I killed Rose because she was trying to steal the love of Uncle Rueben, and I killed Anna because she was going to turn me in for my crimes. Catherine, promise to say the prayers. Report the truth. Set our souls free.

How could this be? Chokecherries? A murder weapon?

The Decision
2012

Catherine paged through what appeared to be Auntie's last family photo album. Most of the pictures were in black and white, and square with notched edges. Auntie used black corners to hold them in place onto the black album pages. She smiled at a photo of her and Auntie sitting beneath the large chokecherry tree in Auntie's yard. By the date imprinted on the side of the photo, Catherine figured she'd been eleven years old. She and Auntie had a large tin pail of chokecherries sitting on either side of them, and they held giant, toothy grins on both their faces.

Catherine refused to accept that such an innocent-looking woman could have been capable of such horrendous crimes. Catherine had only known kindness and love from the woman. What should she do with the knowledge that she had? Does she ruin her aunt's saintly reputation by reporting the truth? Was she obligated to contact the law? Catherine decided the first thing to do was to find out whether chokecherry trees or seeds were, indeed, a poison. Catherine made a call to her mother and offered to take her to her next doctor appointment.

They drove in silence to the clinic, and then Catherine pushed Momma in her noisy wheelchair into the doctor's office. The doctor wanted to check her ears, so he asked Momma to remove her hearing aids. This was Catherine's golden opportunity.

"Doctor, I have a question to ask before she puts her hearing aids back in," she whispered. "I have been looking at some of my family's old, traditional recipes, and I came across one that said chokecherries could be very poisonous. Do you know anything about that?"

"Why, yes," he answered. "In fact, I know of a case where a rancher south of here was accused of having cyanide, but it was during a drought, and it seems the horses began to eat the dried leaves and bark of a chokecherry tree for lack of grass. Normally, an animal instinctively knows to stay away from something that would be harmful, but they must have been hungry. Anyway, the horses died, and when the rancher called out the State Veterinarian, cyanide showed up in the horses' blood. After further investigation, the vet determined it was because of the chokecherry tree's unique drought condition. Be careful when you make that wine or jam, and strain out those seeds. They contain cyanide. I've heard that in the old days, when women strained the juice from the chokecherries, the farmers would use the seeds in their barns for rat and mouse poison."

Seated in Catherine's car, her mother questioned her.

"Now, what were you talking so hush, hush about with the doctor?"

"Nothing, Momma." Catherine clutched the steering wheel of the car while the wheels turned in her own head. "Momma, can you teach me how to make chokecherry jelly?"

Catherine mulled over what to do with the knowledge that she had about Rose's murder. She spent hours searching the Internet about the legal requirements for reporting an old crime, and it didn't appear she had any civic duty to do so. Besides, anyone who would have been connected had long been deceased, and Auntie was still remembered kindly by those still alive in her own family and by the community of St. Giles who knew her. However, Auntie had believed that revealing the truth would have some redemptive value for her soul, and so Catherine reminded herself about the promise she'd made long ago.

Catherine planned to make her final decision after a visit to the St. Mary's Cemetery. She wanted to see the final resting place of young Rose Welsley. As she weaved through rows of scrolled metal crosses, Catherine knelt down to read each name, which was difficult because so many were in German or Norwegian or weren't legible. Finally, she came across a scrolled cross, tipping slightly, and with the effigy of Jesus in the center. Something in German was written below the effigy, and the detail in the cross included beautifully designed roses that weren't on any of the other iron crosses. From the detailed description of the resting place in the newspaper story, Catherine knew she had found the correct grave. She knew Rose couldn't hear her question, but she asked it anyway. "Rose, what should I do? I know Lillian loved you very much. Please forgive her. She was ill. Rest in peace, Rose."

Catherine climbed the steps to the sheriff's department in the Burleigh County Courthouse. She pulled her sweater around her as the rainy afternoon and her reason for being there sent chills through her body. She spoke calmly to the female deputy sitting at the desk. "Good afternoon," she said. "I have come to report a murder."

Epilogue
Rueben and Lillian
1912

Lillian impatiently waited at the front door of her house for Rueben. She noticed his auto drive in from the south. He must have taken the train back to Gwyther from wherever he had been the last two days. The moment he parked next to the mercantile, Lillian stomped over to his automobile door and blocked him from getting out. Her first impulse was to lunge at him and pound her fists into his chest because he did not marry her on Valentine's Day as he had promised. He had shamed her in front of everyone she knew. "Rueben, darling, I was so worried about you," she whimpered. "You left without a word, and I was dressed for our wedding. I would like to know what your excuse is." She fought back the urge to scratch his eyes out.

"Lillian, I think our marriage would be a bad idea right now. I have thought everything through, and I would like to have time to be alone. I have talked to a few of my father's business partners in Bismarck, and they have offered me a handsome sum of money for my property here. I know this little town is your life, so I will make sure that you are taken care of until you marry. Forgive me; I haven't been honest about my feelings for you."

Lillian seethed. She would play her trump card. "Rueben," she said. "I will not consider your offer. Haven't you heard of breach of contract? I want you to know that you are destroying me, and I have questions. Did Ben attend the funeral? Have there been any more clues about what happened to Rose? I was hoping we could have paid our respects *together*, after our wedding. Do you know how hurt I am that I didn't get to attend Rose's funeral?"

"Lillian, I'm going to be perfectly honest with you now. I do not love you. I was using you to help Rose see the mistake that she was making. I have always been in love with Rose, but now she is gone forever. I need to go back to Bismarck because I want justice for Rose. I'm even considering paying for her body to be exhumed after Coroner Kildare returns. I know that with all of Mary's medical bills and the cost of the funeral, Chris Welsley was not in a position to pay for an autopsy."

Standing nearly nose to nose, Lillian glared at Rueben. "Don't do that Rueben. If you do, you'll be digging your own grave. You don't think I didn't know about the little plan you and Rose had concocted?" Lillian sneered. "I knew all along," she said. "Remember, I packed your clothes for the move into my house, and I just happened to pack your vest when a letter fell out with very familiar handwriting. Yes, the handwriting of my best friend in the entire world. When I saw my world falling apart once again, I decided there was only one thing I could do to put it back together. Oh, but I needed your help. You see, I used you, too, Rueben. I used you to deliver a message to Rose, and it was a sweet one at that."

"What in the devil are you talking about? How dare you read my personal mail."

"Yes, it all worked out so well. You were planning to run off with Rose, and you had planned the secret meeting at the boarding house, but you never expected to see her fornicating with Ben. No, not your precious, innocent Rose. In a moment of jealous rage, you calmly served her coffee, and that's one of the things I love about you, Rueben. You have a natural ability to remain calm no matter what, just like now while you destroy me. You knew her weakness was sweets, and you offered her coffee with sugar. There are witnesses. Anna,

Anton, and me, we all saw you spoon out the sugar into her coffee, or at least we saw the sugar bowl next to the cup on the table by the settee. Or was it sugar? I have the sugar bowl, and it was you, Rueben, who killed Rose because she jilted you, and I can prove it."

Rueben knew he was trapped. He didn't have any other choice but to marry Lillian now, and it didn't matter who killed Rose. He appeared to be the most likely suspect. If he had the body exhumed, he would hang, and Lillian would make sure of that. Life really didn't mean anything without Rose, anyway. "Well, then, Lillian, set the date," he said calmly and brushed Lillian aside. He entered the mercantile and slammed the door behind him.

Rueben and Lillian settled into a civil arrangement, and she remembered what Anna had said about the Lakota medicine: It would be powerful if the intentions were good.

Having children, that would be good. Before going to bed on their wedding night, and many nights thereafter, Lillian slipped a potion into Rueben's evening tea. Lillian wondered how long it would take for the aphrodisiac to take effect, but Rueben apparently was not the man she thought he would be.

That was not important. What were important were her life and her self-respect. Maybe someday he would grow to love her. Maybe someday he would even share the marriage bed with her.

As the months went by, Lillian was pleased with the progress Rueben had made with his Catechism studies. She felt fortunate he had completed them and had been baptized before fire destroyed the church. His obedience to Lillian extended to the point of agreeing that they would have their marriage blessed in an appropriate, large wedding ceremony sometime in the future, and all for show, of course. With Lillian's newfound respect through her husband, her parents resumed their relationship with her, and as the years went by, she became a beloved woman in the community. Confession and church became a daily obligation for Lillian, and she knew that Fr. Logan, wherever he was, would have to take her confession of mortal sin with him to the grave, unable to reveal it to anyone but God.

Lillian did not feel guilt for her actions, but she feared Hell. As she aged, she realized that she was not going to be happy on this sinful planet, but she believed that if she could use her power over life and death here on earth, then quite possibly she could find a way to control the destiny of her soul in the next life. Somehow, she would find a way.